VS.
THE BROTHERHOOD

In 1907, a gifted child was kidnapped and taken to a place known as "the Shrine," the ultra-secret headquarters of the sinister "Brotherhood." The child's real name was erased, and he was given the number 13. As memories of his parents faded, he was trained in the arts of power. An exemplary student, he seemed destined to become a great agent of the Brotherhood. Instead, 13 learned the true nature of the Brotherhood, and fled.

Thus began a deadly cat-and-mouse game between Agent 13 and the Brotherhood.

What is the Brotherhood?

The Brotherhood has existed since the dawn of civilization. For millennia, it guided mankind down "the bright path." But then Itsu, the Hand Sinister, seized power and converted light to darkness. Now, in the 1930s, the Brotherhood lusts for global dominance and intends to throw the world into a debilitating war to gain it.

Only Agent 13 stands in their way.

A midnight avenger, Agent 13 is a master of disguise, an invisible operator, and a ruthless destroyer of evil— committed to toppling the Brotherhood through any means. And the Brotherhood fears him, for many of the members have been discovered dead, with the number 13 branded into their foreheads.

Essentially a loner working through a network of informants, Agent 13 has come to trust Maggie Darr, the only person who has seen his real face. Daring and beautiful, Maggie looks as good with a Thompson submachine gun as with a smile. She and 13 are allies, not lovers, but were Agent 13's lifelong mission any less compelling, things might be different. . . .

Join Agent 13 in this fast-paced, action-packed adventure reminiscent of the popular 1930's pulps.

AGENT 13™
THE MIDNIGHT AVENGER

#1

THE INVISIBLE EMPIRE

by **Flint Dille** and **David Marconi**

Cover art by Jeff Butler

TSR, Inc.
PRODUCTS OF YOUR IMAGINATION™

To my sister, Lorraine, and to my mother, Virginia, and to the memory of my father, Robert Dille, all of whom tolerated a lot of ridiculousness while I was learning to be a writer—Flint Dille

To my father, Joseph "Pops" Marconi—David Marconi

AGENT 13™, The Midnight Avenger

Book #1

THE INVISIBLE EMPIRE

© Copyright 1986, Flint Dille and David Marconi. All Right Reserved.

This is a work of fiction. Any resemblance to actual persons, living or dead, is purely coincidental.

This book is protected under the copyright laws of the United States of America. Any reproduction or other unauthorized use of the material or artwork contained herein is prohibited without the express written permission of the copyright holder.

Distributed to the book trade in the United States by Random House, Inc., and in Canada by Random House of Canada, Ltd.

Distributed in the United Kingdom by TSR UK, Ltd.

Distributed to the toy and hobby trade by regional distributors.

AGENT 13 is a trademark owned by Flint Dille and David Marconi

First printing: April 1986
Printed in the United States of America
Library of Congress Catalog Card Number: 86-52197
ISBN: 0-88038-281-3

9 8 7 6 5 4 3 2 1

TSR, Inc.
P.O. Box 756
Lake Geneva, WI 53147

TSR UK, Ltd.
The Mill, Rathmore Road
Cambridge CB1 4AD
United Kingdom

1

INTRIGUE IN ISTANBUL

As the sun sank in the west, long, daggerlike shadows cast by the spiked minarets of Istanbul slid across the Bosporus, foreshadowing the sinister events that darkness would bring.

The noise of honking horns gave way to an impassioned wail to Allah. The people of the day left the streets to the people of the night.

Gypsies danced, as their cooking fires scented the air with exotic spices. Black marketeers lowered their prices and packed their goods, moving quickly to avoid the thieves who drifted from their lairs at night like jackals looking for corpses. Only the self-mutilated beggars remained at their stations, making their final, tearful pleas to the passing strangers for alms to get through the night.

None of this was noticed by the German officer seated comfortably in the back of his Mercedes. The precise, rhythmic purr of the finely tuned engine mellowed the human cacophony into unimportance. The officer stared coldly out the window beyond his chauffeur's shoulder at the colorful crowd that parted like a routed army before his car.

Colonel Schmidt's finger traced the saber slash on his cheek as his steely eyes scanned the streets through the bullet-proof glass. His gaze flicked over the great monuments that stood in ancient, solemn dignity—a marked contrast to the noisy, raucous throng surging around them.

So much for the heart of the proud Byzantine Empire, Schmidt thought. Now the undisciplined masses scurry around this grandeur like rats on a wedding cake. They don't deserve—

"Careful," he murmured as his driver narrowly missed running down a turbanned Sikh who was attempting to cross the street. "We can't be delayed, not tonight."

He eased back into the leather seat, relighting his cigarette. In afterthought, Schmidt mumbled, "I can assure you that these degenerates will be dealt with properly, in due time."

The ambassadorial flags of the Nazi government fluttered defiantly above the gleaming black fenders as the staff-car continued its journey past the Adrianople Gate, the shadow of the Blue Mosque sliding across the hood.

Colonel Schmidt glanced at the passing structure with cynical amusement.

Neither the great religion that built the Mosque, nor the chaotic nation he was visiting, nor even the powerful nation whose black uniform he wore meant anything for him. His duty was to a more ancient cause.

The blood-red sunset silhouetted Hagia Sophia, the church of Constantine, as the Mercedes came to a smooth halt before it. Colonel Schmidt waited as his driver stepped out of the car and scanned the streets for any sign of potential trouble. Seeing none, he opened Schmidt's door.

The German officer emerged, clad in SS black and carrying a heavy briefcase. The driver clicked his heels sharply and saluted. "*Heil* Hitler."

Schmidt glanced at the young officer, smiled sardonically, and walked past without returning the salute.

Private Hadler, the earnest, young Nazi driver, was shocked by the colonel's action. He was proud of his *Fuhrer*, as was all of Germany. It was, after all, Adolf Hitler who had delivered them from the shackles of the Treaty of Versailles, the hated symbol of Germany's humiliation.

Regardless of his vicious tactics, Hitler had restored the German people's national honor—a feat that the regimes of the Weimar Republic had failed to do.

The world again respected Germany. It was Hitler who gave the Germans the strength for equality. It was Hitler who delivered the Rhineland in a bloodless coup, assuring a lasting peace that would sustain the "Thousand Year Reich."

Hitler *deserved* the salute, Hadler thought, especially from an SS colonel. He glared as the colonel entered Hagia Sophia.

What Private Hadler did not know—would never know—was that this colonel was directly responsible for his *Fuhrer*'s rise to power.

"Schmidt" thought about this as he opened the cathedral door and was wrapped in Hagia Sophia's quiet, ancient shadows. In fact, it was the hidden story of that rise to power that was the subject of the report he was about to present to "interested parties." He rehearsed it in his mind as he walked.

"I arrived in Germany during the later part of 1918, one of several agents the Brotherhood had assigned to keep close watch on the various factions vying for control in that defeated, shattered country.

"My orders were to keep a watchful eye on developments in the military. The Brotherhood arranged to have me placed in the Press and News Bureau of the Army's Political Department. We could see that the Army was becoming deeply involved in politics, especially in Bavaria, which was known as an area of staunch conservatism. I suggested that this might be a prime breeding ground for the country's future leaders.

"My investigation uncovered several interesting possibilities. One of these was a young man whose fanatical anti-Semitism seemed likely to appeal to a defeated country looking for a scapegoat. Unfortunately, he had the horrendous name of Schicklgruber. I suggested he change it, and he is now calling himself Hitler—Adolf Hitler.

"With my help and guidance, this Hitler rose to power quickly. We supplied him with a large Swiss bank account, a chauffeured automobile, a villa at Obersalzburg, and a luxurious apartment in Munich. Most impressive to the masses.

"At last I believed it was time to move. Germany was ripe for plucking. I informed the Brotherhood and received permission to topple the Weimar Republic and begin the 'Thousand Year Reich.'

"It was a simple matter to terrify Chancellor von Hindenburg into resigning, thus paving the way for Hitler's grab at the office. Only one stumbling block remained—Austrian Chancellor Dollfuss—and that was easily dealt with.

"We had, of course, made discreet approaches to Dollfuss, but he continued to oppose Hitler publicly. Under my direction, one hundred and fifty-four members of the SS Standart 89 broke into the Federal Chancellery disguised as Austrian Army troops. Dollfuss was arrested and shot.

"There have since been other minor regrettable 'incidents,' but Hitler is now the unquestioned leader of Germany. Germany is now a world power. Hitler is firmly caught in our web. He does not dare make a move without the Brotherhood.

"And now I have been asked to meet with you here, to make my report on Germany's 'readiness.' I can assure you, we are prepared. It is time to take the next step."

Pausing in a corridor, Schmidt checked his surroundings and smiled in satisfaction, then headed for the doorway at the end of the hall.

Light from the dying sun streamed through a window, turning the cold granite walls to a radiant gold. Stepping through the sun-broken shadows, Schmidt made his way to a small chapel now used only for the collection of archaeological artifacts. He stood in the doorway, his hawklike eyes studying the remains of cracked pillars, broken columns, armless statues, and carelessly stored fragmented frescoes.

The German officer's eyes found the object of his search. Walking quickly, he entered a niche nearly obscured by a half-cracked statue of Neptune rising from the sea.

Scanning the room one last time to make certain no tourist was wandering nearby, Schmidt was arrested by a startling sight. Not ten feet from him was a face twisted in pain! Schmidt reached for his P-38, then suddenly stopped.

"It's nothing but a statue," he sneered to himself, trying to halt the surge of adrenaline through his body. He was drawn to look at the statue once again.

It was a life-sized figure of Christ on the cross. And it was terrifyingly lifelike. The anguish in its pain-filled eyes reminded him of his mother—

Resolutely, Schmidt turned away from the Savior's tormented face. Reaching past Neptune into the niche, he pressed on the secret stone. A false wall moved aside, revealing a hidden staircase. He was just about to step inside when he felt himself irresistibly compelled to look back at the statue. Something was odd.... Those eyes ... life-like ... burning ...

Suddenly, the Savior's hand moved. Pulling one of the "nails" from the cross, the "statue" flung it through the air.

Schmidt gasped, but before he could react, the throwing knife buried itself in his neck. The German pitched to the floor, twisting in death's final spasms. His last impression before the pain exploded his brain was of the figure of Christ descending from the cross....

Still covered in alabaster-colored paint, the killer knelt by the German's side and lifted the man's hand. There was no pulse.

For all the expression that crossed his face, the killer might well have been a statue. He struck a large ring he wore against the stone floor. The room suddenly filled with a sizzling, magnesium-white light. The killer pressed the glowing ring to the dead German's forehead. There was a hissing sound and the smell of burning flesh.

When the killer raised the ring from the German's flesh, a message was left behind—the number 13.

Agent 13 wiped the marblelike make-up from his face. It was a handsome face, or might have been but for the cold, remorseless eyes—the eyes of a trained assassin. He felt no pangs of con-science. He had been trailing this man for four months—four months while the numbers of those murdered by the German stretched into the hun-dreds. Now Schmidt himself was dead. The world was, by a small measure, a better place.

Turning from the body, Agent 13 slit open the German's briefcase. As expected, it was booby-trapped to go off if the wrong man opened it. With a skilled motion, he disarmed the ticking weapon.

In almost the same motion, he pulled out of the case what appeared to be the purple, velvet robes of a monk. Beneath the robes were several manila file folders. A quick glance showed Agent 13 the nature and importance of their contents.

One dealt with German troop strengths and locations. One contained a detailed synopsis of Hitler's game plan for the war. There were many folders like these. But tucked in among them, almost as if in afterthought, was another folder that had—seemingly—nothing to do with the war. It was a dossier on an American scientist by the name of Dr. David Fischer.

Secreting the files in a hidden location in the chapel where he could pick them up later, Agent 13 robed himself in the purple vestments. He then slid through the hidden door behind Neptune, a door that few knew even existed. Closing it softly behind him, 13 silently descended a narrow flight of winding stairs into a dark and mysterious part of Hagia Sophia.

In the fourth century A.D., palace intrigue threatened the Byzantine Empire. Needing a safe place to forge secret treaties, the bishops and pro-consuls developed plans to construct a chamber beneath the church, only to discover, upon investigation, that one already existed.

It had been built nearly a thousand years earlier by the Thracian king, Bizas, whose pagan symbols still adorned the walls. Gratefully taken over by the Byzantines, the chamber was—after conquest of Byzantium by the Moors and then the Turks—forgotten.

Forgotten, that is, by all save the Brotherhood.

This night, after hundreds of years of dusty solitude, the chamber of King Bizas was once more inhabited. Several figures dressed in purple, hooded robes stood together in the light shed by flickering torches. Their identities were concealed from each other by the hooded garb. Of all different nationalities, many had traveled a long way to come and receive their next instructions.

Though each spoke a different native tongue, all joined their voices in the recitation of ancient rites in a language lost to scholars over three thousand years ago.

When the rites were concluded, the torches were snuffed. A chill, damp darkness settled over the chamber. Into the silence came the sound of rock moving on rock. A cold draft whistled through the room, a new light flared. The waiting robed figures slowly turned toward the open secret panel.

Another cowled and robed figure—masked like all the others—stood outlined in a faint greenish glow. A sigh of anticipation whispered through the robed figures as they bowed in homage. "A Rook!" they murmured, impressed.

And now they knew why this meeting had been called. If the masked figure had been a Knight, tonight's gathering would have concerned the infiltration of military or industrial targets. A Bishop might mean Rome was ripe and ready to fall. But a Rook! Rooks resided at the Shrine itself, taking their orders directly from Itsu—the Hand Sinister. With armies mobilized on every border in Europe, this Rook need only cry havoc to let slip the dogs of war.

The Rook's hand went to a large, round amulet hanging from a chain around his neck. With fingers as thin and deadly as the legs of a poisonous spider, the man raised the pendant to one eye.

With no word spoken, the robed figures raised their right hands, palms outward. The Rook looked at each palm through the stone in the pendant. A tattooed number appeared on each palm, framed by the ancient symbol of Omega. Invisible to all save the user of the Seer Stone, the numbers served to identify the figures before him as members of the Brotherhood.

"39," he whispered, "19, 82, 13—"

13!

There was a sudden flare of torchlight, a strange spraying sound, and a noxious green cloud began to fill the room.

Clutching their throats, the robed figures dropped to the floor. Within seconds, nothing moved. The green cloud hung in the damp air, glimmering in the torchlight.

Then the green cloud swirled as another robed figure made its way toward the Rook. The figure bent down and pried the man's fingers loose from the Seer Stone, which he clutched tightly, even in death. The robed figure dropped the Seer Stone into a pocket. Then there was the sound of metal striking rock, a brilliant white light, and the smell of burning flesh.

Half an hour later, a turbanned old man in muslin robes emerged from an alleyway near the dock. The low wail of a ship's horn filled the air, signaling final boarding. The man walked swiftly, heading for a beat-up old freighter that lay at anchor between the brooding darkness of the Black Sea and the soft sea of Marmara.

As the man passed, he tossed an object into the water. The gas mask sank quickly.

Satisfied, he continued on his way, scurrying up the gangplank of the departing ship. Soon the man would be safely through the Dardanelles and into the Aegean Sea.

Only the grimly marked corpses were left behind, evidence that Agent 13 had struck again!

THE INVISIBLE EMPIRE

In 452 A.D., the Scourge of God, Attila the Hun, led his barbaric army toward the gates of Rome. As the Mongol horsemen eagerly advanced to sack the city, they were stopped by a strange and beautiful scene. Looking almost dreamlike in the misty light, Pope Leo I and two of his cardinals rode toward the thundering horde.

Dark-haired Huns raised their small horse-bows, but, at a gesture from their khan, they lowered their weapons. Leaning close to Attila's ear, the white-robed pontiff whispered a few words and—the Holy City was spared.

History has lost the words spoken by the Pope.

History has also lost any knowledge of the two men who really saved the Roman Empire . . . except in one place, where their memories are revered.

One of Rome's saviors was an obscure cardinal, attending (supposedly) His Holiness. The other was one of the maji, serving (ostensibly) Attila.

In the darkness of an early morning two months before Attila's arrival near Rome, both the magus and cardinal received whispered messages, delivered secretly by spectral figures. The two were instructed to stop the invasion.

On receiving this command, from a leader more powerful than any these two ostensibly served, the two set to work.

Before Attila's forces reached Rome's gate, their khan called a meeting of all his spiritual advisors, seeking holy guidance for his final assault on the city.

The oil lamps burned late in the tent of the Great One, as the Ten Magi gathered. One by one, they moved forward and offered their words and visions. Soon, only one remained to speak. He was tall, emaciated, and old. His ancient, withered hands clutched a crusted leather sack. All eyes in the room turned to him expectantly.

"Speak," commanded Attila in a voice that would send most men to their knees, cowering for their lives.

The Old One moved slowly to the center of the tent. Opening the sack, he spread the contents on a small floor tapestry. Attila leaned forward, looking. They were goat entrails.

Studying the entrails for "a sign," the magus gave Attila his reading.

It was a warning. Should Attila ever meet a man in white accompanied by two in red, he must do whatever deed the man in white asked of him. Failure to obey the conditions of the prophecy would result in the Great One's painful death on the tip of a Roman spear and a pestilence upon his kingdoms—the horror of which the world had never known.

The Pope, meanwhile, was told by the cardinal of a "vision" indicating that His Holiness would have the power to turn the pagan horde if he but rode out to face them, accompanied by only two cardinals. All His Holiness need do was speak with the Hun's leader, telling him to leave the city, and the Lord would undertake to see that His Servant was obeyed.

Thus, when the Pope told Attila to turn his horsemen away from Rome, he did so—quickly!

The old magus and the cardinal, though loyal to their respective camps, both secretly served a more eternal and ancient power—the Brotherhood.

From its inception in the ruins of the once-great civilization of Lemuria, the Brotherhood had acted in the cause of good. Its deeds were not measured in flamboyant actions or bold strokes, but rather in silence—wars that were never fought, wicked kings who never ruled, plagues that never spread, famines that never blighted the land.

Using secrecy as a protective shield from the masses who might seek to corrupt their noble mission, the organization acted quietly, an unseen, benevolent hand guiding world events.

When it was decided, for example, that mankind had learned the lessons taught by the darkness of the Middle Ages, an order was issued to take humankind to the next level.

The Brotherhood's scholars began their task. Working from sacred texts (believed by most to have been destroyed in the burning of the library at Alexandria) and the Crystals of Uru—whose powerful, mystic forces as well as the knowledge contained within the Crystals themselves predated even their own organization—the Brotherhood injected the sweet nectar of renaissance into the fevered body of a dark age.

Soon the great wind of enlightenment swept across civilization. Even the church's high dogma fell prey to the new light.

Thus it was that the Invisible Hand guided human destiny for so long. And thus it would have continued were it not for universal and immutable laws that balance light with darkness, pleasure with pain, love with hate, and good with evil.

Whether power corrupts or corruption seeks

power is a debate for philosophers. Suffice it to say that the august body of the Brotherhood, after centuries of vitality, began to rot from within.

The Invisible Hand grew sharp talons, and the All Seeing Eye took on a sinister gleam.

Slowly, the precepts of goodness were bent to become the precepts of evil, and the line between purity and abomination disappeared.

Slowly, the Invisible Hand reached for the throat of mankind.

As a cancer of an entire body starts with one cell, the shadow of one being fell upon all.

For it was the Hand Sinister, known long ago as Itsu, who seized the Crystals' knowledge for himself—for eternity.

Months after the carnage in Istanbul, the grim murder scene was restaged in the Hand Sinister's secret chamber. After each of the Brotherhood's agents dropped to the floor in mock death, and the actor playing Agent 13 slipped away, the Hand Sinister sat alone upon the throne.

Alone, the physical embodiment of Cheated Death and Tainted Life took a deep breath that sounded like the mountain winds of Tibet. He closed his eyes and began to meditate. Deeply entranced, he created a plan to accomplish three objectives:

One, he must regain the Seer Stone.

Two, he must cause a torrent of death to fall from the clouds of war that loomed over the Earth.

Three, he must bring cold silence to Agent 13.

In the calm of darkness, a plot slowly began to form. A beautiful woman . . . a ruthless man . . . the Four Primal Fears: Falling, the Dark, Fire . . . He would leave the fourth Fear for later. Yes . . .

In his isolation, the Hand Sinister smiled.

LIGHTNING STRIKES

It was unseasonably warm for October. A fair wind blew off the Atlantic, and many of the spectators had either opened or removed the heavy wool coats they had carried with them to the Maryland shore.

Before them was a scene that might have been the work of surrealistic artists. A surplus tank from the Great War stood on a decorated platform constructed near the crashing surf. Fifty yards away, three soldiers stood guard around four portable generators, which were all connected with electrical umbilical cords to a gigantic, six-foot-high gun.

But this gun was no ordinary hulking cannon of iron. No, this gun was built of glass tubes, conductors, amplifiers, and dials. Colored gases filled some of the tubes, while a vivid blue glow pulsed in the large, coiled, central tube. The device hummed audibly, as though pregnant with power.

A small observation area had been set up on a low hill overlooking the beach. Its weary white folding chairs were filled by military men and politicians, two of whom were reputed to be very "close" to the President—General Braddock, aging head of the Joint Chiefs of Staff, and a newcomer to the political field—Kent Walters, head of the powerful National Security Council.

In addition to the "elite" in the white chairs, reporters crowded around the demonstration area, continuously clicking cameras at the strange-looking contraption, as if it might have moved.

One reporter wearing a white driving cap took a quick swig of brandy from his hip flask, then offered it to the much taller reporter next to him, who waved it off.

"Well, whaddaya think, Eddie?" Corbett, the short one, asked, pocketing his flask.

"I'm sorry the baseball season's over," Eddie said with a laugh.

"You can say that again. Think the Giants'll do it next year?"

"Naw, go with the Dodgers," Eddie Faulk said in a bored tone. Then he turned toward the shore as the aging General Braddock stepped behind a lectern set between the viewing area and the strange gun.

"Good afternoon, gentlemen." His voice crackled. He fiddled with the microphone and then began again. "As most of you know, I am General Hunter Braddock. Today, we are gathered to witness the demonstration of a weapon that may revolutionize warfare. Its inventor, Dr. David Fischer, calls it—somewhat dramatically—the 'Lightning Gun.' I'm sure that the military would call it something dashing like the 'L-976.' " Braddock paused as the audience dutifully laughed and then went on. "The weapon's inventor is with us today to explain how it works. Dr. Fischer."

A slender, gray man stepped in front of the assembled soldiers, politicians, and reporters.

What a sad case of a man, Faulk thought.

Nature had tricked the scientist into accepting a physique so frail that even the activity of walking demanded full attention. In addition, he had a face so joyless that it was impossible to imagine it breaking out into a full smile.

"What you are about to see is a demonstration of my latest prototype of the Directed Electricity Weapon, known also, as General Braddock has already pointed out, as the 'Lightning Gun.'

"Although I cannot, of course, give you the details of design, I would just like to point out that this test weapon today is powered by only the relatively small generators that you see before you. Therefore it will have a relatively low yield.

"It is my intention, should I receive the funding I have requested, to build a much larger Lightning Gun, whose magnitude and yield would be up to fifty times that which you will see today. Various sized versions could be mounted on everything from flat-bed trucks to battleships. I think I am not being immodest when I say that this weapon could revolutionize the concept of battle."

There was a slight murmur from the crowd.

"Now, if you would all please put on the protective goggles you have been given, we will get on with the demonstration." Fischer stepped away from the lectern. His shoulders slumped as if in relief at being out of the limelight.

General Braddock made a gesture to the three soldiers, who moved into action.

As preparations were being made, Eddie Faulk, the tall reporter, scanned the crowd. His eyes were not those of a journalist but of a secret avenger locked in a deadly battle with the forces of darkness. For Eddie Faulk was none other than Agent 13.

13 knew he was not alone in posing as something he wasn't. Almost certainly, one of the other observers was a member of the Brotherhood. This much he had learned from the papers taken from the dead German's briefcase. Colonel Schmidt

had been planning to attend this demonstration. He wouldn't now, of course, but some other member must be here. But who?

The Agent eyed the crowd, but it was a futile gesture and he knew it. It could be one of the soldiers operating the gun. It might be the private who had escorted him to the press area. It might be General Braddock himself.

A moment later, Agent 13's thoughts were jarred by a harsh command.

"READY!"

The Agent, putting on his goggles, saw the soldiers point the strange weapon at the tank.

"AIM!"

They made their final adjustments, then turned their heads, shielding their goggle-covered eyes.

"FIRE!"

A soldier manning the generators threw a switch. A sizzling buzz pierced the air and a blinding flash issued from the gun.

Then, bolts of light, like many whips all cracked by the same master, slammed into the tank.

BLAAAM!

The tank blew. An orange ball of flame rose in the sky. Large chunks of metal flew in all directions. There was a loud cheer and a round of applause from the crowd.

The reporters removed their goggles and ran toward the smoldering heap, cameras clicking.

Agent 13 ran with them, his note pad under his arm, and his camera held ready.

"Yah ask me, I think it's a fraud," Corbett offered from beside Eddie Faulk, who was diligently clicking off frames. "I think there was dynamite inside that thing all along. Military snake oil. Just another way to pry long green out of John Q. Public."

13 didn't reply, but he did surreptitiously exam-

ine the rubble for signs that the other reporter's suspicion might be right. There was no trace or smell of the cordite associated with powder blasts. Only the lingering smell of ozone from an electrical arc. The weapon had clearly caused the incredible destruction.

"Well, whaddaya think, Faulk?" Corbett persisted, tugging on his driving cap.

"Damnedest thing I've ever seen," Faulk muttered finally. He didn't have to pretend the amazed tone in his voice—13 was truly astounded by the damage the gun had done.

"Well, I'm not supportin' it. The last thing we need is some expensive new toy for the Army."

Faulk didn't answer. The Lightning Gun hadn't worked like any weapon 13 had ever seen before. It hadn't blown up its target—the gas in the tank had done that. What it appeared to have done was infuse so much energy into the tank that it had blown out every individual rivet, cooked every wire, and set fire to every object within. It was clearly a weapon of mass destruction.

Agent 13 turned and eyed Dr. Fischer, who stood surrounded by reporters. He had shed his natural timidity in this moment of scientific glory.

Two things were certain—the Brotherhood was interested in this weapon, and they must not be allowed to get their hands on it. But a weapon this powerful could be used as a means of maintaining peace as well as fighting a war. If the United States military was truly interested in developing the Lightning Gun for its own use, America's position would be strengthened dramatically.

Dr. Fischer would have to be watched—closely. If the Brotherhood made a move for him, he would have to be rescued and removed from danger. Or, if that proved impossible, the scientist would have to be destroyed—along with his prototype gun, his notes, everything.

Suddenly, 13's thoughts were jerked back to his surroundings by Corbett, the short reporter, tugging on his sleeve.

"Hey, Faulk! Get a load of that!"

A black limousine with a police cherry on top was screaming toward the shore where the observers were still milling around the tank remnants. Immediately, the senior government official present—Kent Walters, the National Security Advisor—ran toward it.

The Agent was among the reporters who dashed along behind Walters toward the limo. Something was up. Something that concerned the National Security Advisor. Everyone was speculating. Could it be war?

By the time 13 reached the limousine, guards had closed in behind the National Security Advisor. Faulk was, after all, just another reporter.

The reporters clamored around the limo, demanding answers to shouted questions while the guards shoved them back. Agent 13's hearing had been trained many years ago to receive and decipher specific noises from the midst of chaos. He focused his attention on Kent Walters, who was speaking to his aide. The fragments of conversation that 13 overheard alarmed him. Elbowing his way past a shouting cameraman, he managed to hear one final bit before the car door slammed shut.

"Set up a meeting of the National Security Council. We'll screen it there! America *will not* be blackmai—"

"Whaddaya think, Faulk?" asked Corbett. But the tall reporter was busy watching the black limo disappear down the road, speeding toward Washington.

THE CRYPTIC TRYST

The brightly lit Capitol dome glowed against the dark, satiny night. To some, that dome was a beacon of freedom in the murk of growing global tyranny. To others, it was the glowing heart of a benevolent empire. But to Agent 13, observing the gleaming dome through a filthy window in a deserted warehouse, it was an egg about to be knocked from its safe and secure wall. In the autumn of 1937, America's isolationist shell was thin, easily cracked.

When Japanese bombers sank the American gunboat *Panay* in the Yangtze River, few Americans felt that the growling Eastern Empire had anything to do with them.

In a vain effort to avoid entanglement in the impending global war, the U.S. House and Senate ratified three successive Neutrality Acts in 1935, '36, and '37. Even so, the harder the young democracy tried to isolate herself from world affairs, the farther she was drawn into them.

But she faced a worse danger still, though only one man knew of it—the Brotherhood. After viewing the havoc wrought by war-breeding incidents in Europe and Asia, Agent 13 knew that the Brotherhood's next efforts would be directed here—against the Great Democracy. Agent 13 knew he had to stop them . . . but his position was weak.

His adventure in Istanbul had been a trade-off. Killing the Rook and the German in Istanbul had dealt a devastating blow to the Brotherhood—they would have to find and train a new mentor for their Hitler, and they would be forced to make some time-consuming leadership changes. But it had also severed 13's most important link to the organization.

Still, he had deemed it necessary and now he did not regret his actions—he had the Seer Stone, and with it he could identify any member of the Brotherhood. As long as he had it, the Brotherhood was vulnerable. The Istanbul incident had also revealed the Brotherhood's interest in this Dr. Fischer and his Lightning Gun, an interest that boded well for no one.

No, it had been worth the risk. With the Seer Stone he had the means to destroy the Brotherhood by having the capability to uncover any member. 13 knew that the Brotherhood would stop at nothing to get the pendant back. Therefore, he would use it as bait to bring the most powerful secret society in history down upon him. And thus, he hoped to be able find and destroy their leaders.

It was a risk, but there was no choice, not with the Brotherhood's interest in the Lightning Gun, although Agent 13 was, at the moment, at a loss to see how it might be useful to them. But then, there had never been a choice. Life or death—those were his stakes. Those had been his stakes ever since severing his own bonds with the ancient organization half a lifetime ago.

Closing his eyes, Agent 13 "saw" the Hand Sinister, the Brotherhood's ruler, as he had heard him described:

A gaunt face . . . burning eyes. "They will drive you mad if you stare into them. . . ." A hawk nose

. . . chiseled teeth . . . yellowed skin creased by a thousand wrinkles . . . "He's been kept alive for millennia on infant's blood and jackal's bane. . . ." The haunting face . . . laughing . . . ancient, rotted breath blowing upon the victim . . .

Then he saw himself at a chessboard, sitting across from the Hand Sinister. Agent 13 made a clever move and a "rook" died among the minarets of Istanbul. Reality within abstraction. Now the shadow of a skeletal hand again hovers above the board, reaching down. . . .

Then, twisting his mind around like a metaphysical Moebius strip, he looked at the board through the eyes of his enemy. Hearing laughter echoing in the ancient skull, peering through ancient eye sockets, he saw the Dead German and the Living Agent 13. . . .

A horrifying possibility broke over him! The Hand Sinister had *sacrificed* the Nazi! It was all part of a scheme as involved as the pattern in a Turkish rug, but he could see only the very edge, the fringes of a scheme within a plot within a battle within a war within an imperial ambition whose complexity was so great that none save the Hand Sinister could grasp it.

13 pounded his fist on a table as—

The phone rang.

He lifted the receiver but did not speak. Customary procedure. His colleagues knew that familiar silence better than their mothers' voices.

"The eyes of—uh—the—uh—Owl see in—uh—many directions."

"Proceed," said 13, smiling slightly.

"The—uh—Falconers con-congregate in . . . damn it! Lemme tell ya straight, boss."

"Go ahead, Benny." He knew what the call was about. The code wasn't necessary for this. Though a trusted informer, Benny had his intellectual limits.

"That meetin' ya wanted to know about. It's tonight at eight."

"Where?"

"All I could get was that it's in some place called 'Eagle's Nest.' That a tavern?"

"Thank you. Now, I want you to tail a man named Fischer, David Fischer. He can be found in the Physics Laboratories at Wilber University. I want to know who he sees and where he goes."

"Gotcha. Anythin' else?"

"No." The line went dead.

Benny the Eye—a member of 13's organization. In the course of his relentless battle with the Brotherhood, the Agent had pulled many lives from the dark shadow cast by that ancient evil. Some of those he saved volunteered their lives to his service, so, in time, he had built up a strong network of agents from all walks of life: police, criminals, sports figures, actors, politicians.

Benny was an odd case. A completely nondescript little man, he had the priceless ability to fade into the woodwork. Thus, Benny the Eye could go anywhere, see all, and hear all—without being noticed. He was also the best "tail" in the business.

Acting on the words Agent 13 had heard National Security Advisor Kent Walters say at the Lightning Gun test, he had put his best operative on the trail, and now it had paid off.

The National Security Council, made up of America's top lawmen, was meeting in emergency session tonight in their secret headquarters.

Had the Hand Sinister made his move?

DEATH'S CALLING CARDS

Thousands of Washingtonians drove past the National Security building daily without having any idea of what went on inside. It could have passed for an embassy or even the home of one of the remaining "old" families of Washington. But, in fact, it was the arm of the U.S. Government that attempted to fill the gap between national law enforcement, the State Department, and the War Department.

The midnight oil burned late in a room on the top floor camouflaged as a luxurious penthouse apartment. Inside, behind thick, flowered curtains, a movie projector's beam of light cut through thick cigar smoke that hung motionless in the darkened room. Five men were seated at a massive oak table strewn with file folders. Their attention was focused on the film's images unrolling on the screen at the far end of the room.

Each of the men whose faces flickered in the light of the projector represented a different facet of American law. Together, they made up the National Security Countil.

Assistant Attorney General John Myerson was the horse trader. The slightly overweight politician, who had risen to his position through shrewd and cunning deals made with little fish in order to hook big fish, sat in a leather armchair, puffing on his cigar as he watched the film with a bored expression.

Next to him sat Jack Halloran of Treasury. Strong-jawed, bald as a cue ball, Halloran was a pure-strain gumshoe more at ease on the streets than in a plush penthouse. He invariably rolled a silver dollar over his finger knuckles, no matter where he was or what he was doing.

Kent Walters, the National Security Advisor, was the stoic frontier marshal. A born leader, he had no patience for details and, as an administrator, he didn't need any. All he needed to do was raise posses and chase after the bad guys. Given his quick rise out of the East Coast political machine, he apparently did that quite well. A shrewd judge of character, he was also gifted with a knack for making the right call, especially when it came to events of world-wide importance. Having already seen the film, he watched his deputies more closely than the screen.

Next to him sat Constantin Gyrakos, head of the East Coast division of the Secret Service. Gyrakos was the plodding investigator. "The old man of the department," Constantin had seen and experienced it all, often relating his stories with a dry, biting humor.

The last person in the room was Robert Buckhurst, Deputy Director of the FBI. Dr. Buckhurst sat in his tweed suit, puffing on a severe pipe that dangled from his lower lip. The "modern scientist" of the group, hand-picked by Hoover to be here, Buckhurst viewed himself as the future of law enforcement. Never one to make a rash or hasty decision before all the evidence and possible angles had been explored, he sat in a cold, unmoving silence.

No one sat too near Buckhurst. He was neither liked nor trusted. Everybody knew that whatever was said in his presence went straight back to his boss. But tonight, this was his show.

All eyes, except Walters's, were on the screen, viewing a spectacle both horrifying in image and implication. The gaping maw of a railroad tunnel spat out the *Olympian,* a thundering locomotive. Smoke and steam poured from its mighty stack, sparks shot from the track, and the shriek of a whistle whined through a desolate Montana valley.

One by one, train cars emerged from the tunnel. The first five held passengers, then came a pair of box cars, and finally, tank cars, with the word "HELIUM" painted on the side.

The locomotive roared onto a 180-foot-high trestle bridge that stretched across Custer Creek Canyon like a spider web made of steel.

Suddenly, an explosion shook the trestles. The bridge crumbled as if made of matchsticks. With a wailing shriek of its whistle, like a dying scream, the train plunged into the chasm. Almost simultaneously, the cars carrying the helium cracked open, releasing the liquid to the open air, where hundreds of tons of the valuable substance immediately disappeared into the atmosphere.

As the train dropped into the canyon like a bizarre, reticulated snake, Myerson shifted his heavy girth and muttered through his soggy cigar, "The Montana Line crash . . ."

"I still say that crash was an accident," injected Gyrakos. "A flash flood weakened the bridge. . . ."

"Then who the hell took this movie?" Walters turned to Buckhurst. "What did Hoover's boys find out?"

Buckhurst answered coldly and precisely. "The footage was taken with a wide-angle lens from a low-flying aircraft of unknown type and origin flying approximately twelve hundred feet above the train with an airspeed of sixty knots. None of the survivors reported hearing or seeing an aircraft at any time before, during, or after the crash.

"I considered the possibility that the aircraft had dropped a bomb on the train and had several forensic experts in my lab check the film frame by frame. The first explosion was on the bridge, the next two on the train, though the helium itself, of course, could not explode. It leads me to believe that they were set off by some type of remote control—perhaps activated from the aircraft or somewhere nearby—or even by the train itself—a pressure mine on the tracks, a trip timer with a fuse, or any of a dozen other ways. It's impossible to tell at this time."

The images on the screen changed suddenly, pulling back the men's attention.

This time, the scene was of a distant factory in a desert. Several experimental-type fighter planes sat on a nearby airstrip. A high security fence surrounded the entire complex. At one security post, three guards could be seen idly chatting in the midday sun. All appeared calm and orderly. And then—

A massive explosion ripped through the factory, sending chunks of steel, airplanes, men, and cement-block wall upward in a growing, smoke-filled tower of debris. Moments later, the shock waves from the massive explosion knocked the guards off their feet, soon shaking even the camera itself, as evidenced by the jittery movement of the image. Then, only spiraling smoke and raining debris filled the screen.

Buckhurst knew what his colleagues' questions would be. "The footage was taken with a telephoto lens from the Lone Steer Cafe, an abandoned structure approximately one thousand yards from the northern perimeter fence of Westron Aircraft—"

"You mean what used to be Westron Aircraft,"

grunted Gyrakos, the joker.

Eyeing him disapprovingly, Buckhurst continued, "The destruction was total. More then sixteen hundred cubic feet of ground composition
was displaced. The resulting crater was approximately seventeen feet deep and fifty feet in diame-
ter at the surface."

"Those guys didn't have a chance," mumbled
Halloran, his silver coin shining in the light as he
flicked it faster and faster.

"Any aircraft seen in the area?" asked Walters.

"Not that's been reported so far," Buckhurst
replied, coughing slightly and glancing irritably
at Myerson and his eternal cigar. "Once again, we
believe that the bomb was activated by remote
control. Shortly before the explosion occurred,
one of the guards along the northern fence
remembered seeing a brown Ford pickup truck
pull into the Lone Steer Cafe with steam pouring
out of its engine. The driver climbed out, lifted the
hood, and appeared to be making some repairs to
the steaming engine. It was at this time that the
explosion occurred. Several minutes later, the
driver, seemingly terror-stricken, jumped into the
truck and fled."

"Did he get a make on the guy?" demanded
Myerson.

"No," replied Buckhurst. "The driver was too
far away for the guard to identify. But two days
later, the burned-out remains of a truck fitting the
description was found in the desert forty miles
from the factory. A clean white sheet of paper was
on the charred seat inside the cab, and embossed
on it was the symbol you'll find black-and-white
glossy prints of in the folders in front of you."

Leafing through his folder, Myerson found the
desired print. He pulled it out and studied the
symbol.

"It is the symbol Omega," continued Buckhurst. "Experts on these things have been unable to attach it to any known organization."

"What does it mean?" demanded Halloran.

"The end."

Myerson snorted. "The end of what?"

"Just 'the end,'" Buckhurst said with an edge of finality. "There were no words, no demands, only the symbol. As for the truck itself, the license plates and engine serial numbers had been removed."

"Untraceable?" queried Myerson, snubbing out his cigar.

"Thus far. What my men found even stranger was that there was no sign of anyone or anything leaving the wreck, though there'd been no wind or rain for days. The sand was smooth, blank. No foot or tire prints to be seen anywhere nearby." Buckhurst raised his hand as a signal for the projectionist to continue.

"Sounds like your boys have had their hands full," remarked Walters, his attention again shifting to the screen.

This time it was a more familiar image—the dirigible *Hindenburg,* the pride of the German airship fleet, slowly settling to its mooring-mast at Lakehurst, New Jersey. The film was being shot by someone standing in the crowd on the ground. Suddenly, the blurred image of a woman's large hat filled the screen.

As the shot was brought into focus, the intricate beadwork design encircling the hat came into focus. The design was the same Omega symbol found in the pickup. Her 'message' delivered, the well-dressed woman disappeared back into the crowd, her face hidden by the large hat bearing the symbol. The film shifted its focus back to the *Hindenburg*, just in time to see it burst into flames. Slowly the inferno spread, engulfing the huge ship as it fell, fatally stricken, to the ground.

"Just after the disaster, we questioned the ground crew and the people who had been waiting for arriving passengers." Buckhurst's voice was clinical in its detachment. "There were several people taking motion pictures of the landing. We've checked all of them out—they're all legit. Besides, none of them had cameras nearly sophisticated enough for this film. We believe that someone hidden in a service vehicle parked in the area took the motion picture—same method as was used at the Westron Factory."

"The cause?" asked Gyrakos, though his tone said he already knew the answer.

"After examining the film, we once again believe it was a bomb, planted in the *Hindenburg* before its departure from Frankfurt. The device probably exploded near one of the rear gas bags of the ship. It wouldn't take much—hydrogen's so combustible the littlest spark would set it off."

Walters asked Buckhurst, "What do the Germans think?"

"I sent them the information on the other disasters and we're still waiting for their experts to give us their opinions. Off the record, they appear to be as confused as we are, but, seeing all the enemies they've been creating lately, I'm sure they have ideas of their own. . . ."

A figure slowly superimposed itself over the image of the flaming *Hindenburg*. The figure wore a hood over its head. The only features of the face visible through the mask were a pair of cold eyes and lips, whose skin was parched and cracked. The

Omega symbol found in the burned-out truck and seen at the *Hindenburg* disaster was seen once more—now affixed to the center of the cloth hood. An evenly measured, sinister voice began to speak as the airship continued to burn.

"Gentlemen, what you have just witnessed is only a sample of the disasters that I, the Masque, am capable of causing. They are but a hint of the horrors that will befall the United States and other countries if my demands are not met.

"My present demands are as follows: First, weapons research and production at the Taylor, McVickers, Bearings, and Thompson plants will be stopped immediately.

"Second, 'Operation Seahawk'—the naval exercise scheduled to take place in the Caribbean next month—will be canceled.

"Third, all work and research relating to the *Essex* and *Atlanta* class warships will be discontinued immediately.

"Fourth and finally, for the time being, the Naval Research Laboratory will be disbanded. All its scientists and personnel will be filtered back into civilian life."

After a pause, the sinister figure continued, "We can strike anywhere at any time. You and your armies are powerless to stop us. My demands, like my disasters, are easy to understand. You have one week to respond. If you intend to comply, I'll expect to see a red flare glowing over the Treasury Building in Washington, D.C., precisely at midnight on October 20. Failure to do so will set off disasters of even greater magnitude.

"Do not test my patience, gentlemen—"

Halloran turned to Buckhurst. "This is the fifth time we've seen this. That's enough."

Buckhurst turned and signaled the projectionist in the back of the room. "That'll be all for tonight, thank you." The projector ground to a halt as the lights came back up in the smoke-filled room.

Several of the men, blinking in the sudden light, looked at the large wall clock in the corner of the room. The time was 11:35 p.m.

Buckhurst puffed on his pipe, bringing a reddened glow to the cherry tobacco. "I wish I had better news, but as you can see, thus far we haven't come up with anything of much use."

"What about the clown in the hooded mask?" demanded Gyrakos with a gruff Bogart tone.

"Nothing. We've had linguistics experts, trying to detect a regional accent or something, but there's nothing. We even sent film samples to all the major development labs, hoping they could help us trace it to the processor. Again nothing."

Buckhurst turned to Myerson. "What did the Attorney General say?"

Myerson, stuffing papers back into his folder, said, "He talked to the President himself. Roosevelt refuses to budge. Under no circumstances will he compromise our national security and give in to the demands. They view the problem as ours, and they expect results!"

Halloran looked at the clock, watching as the final moments ticked by. "Well, then it looks like we're going to have to ride out the storm."

Gyrakos shifted nervously in his seat. "The deadline expires in fifteen minutes." Standing suddenly, he walked to a window and opened it. In the far distance the lights atop the Treasury Building glowed and somewhere beyond that glowed the eyes of a fiend, waiting for a signal that would never come.

From behind them came a voice.

"You are fools to underestimate the danger the United States is in. Yet you would also be fools to submit to it."

VOICE FROM THE SHADOWS

Gyrakos spun around. Standing directly behind him was the projectionist, a nondescript, middle-aged man with a receding hairline and rumpled clothing.

"When we need a projectionist's advice, we'll ask for it," snarled Myerson, glancing at the man irritably. "Meanwhile, you're through for tonight. Just get the hell out—"

But Gyrakos made an abrupt cutting motion with his hand. "Wait a minute. Something about this guy's not right," he said evenly. "Look at his eyes."

Every man in the room turned his attention on the projectionist, who was nodding and smiling grimly, letting his gaze sweep over them in turn. He held no weapon—unless it *was* that strange, intense look in his eyes.

"Mr. Walters, move your hand away from your pocket, or I'll be forced to kill you."

Walters did as he was told. The others instinctively placed their hands on the table, attesting to their lack of weapons. The air of danger in the room was palpable.

The projectionist continued speaking. "I am Agent 13. You all have heard of me, and you all have different opinions of me. Some are accurate, others are not, but whatever you think of me or my motives, have no doubt that I am your ally against the Masque."

The Agent, with extensive files on these men, knew what each was thinking.

Buckhurst (and thereby the FBI) had no evidence to prove the Agent's existence; therefore, the Assistant Director believed 13 did not exist. But Buckhurst was, of course, willing to listen, filing everything away in his head to report to J. Edgar.

Walters, whose overheard words at the Fischer demonstration had led the Agent to this meeting, regarded Agent 13 with an icy calm, perhaps looking for the flaw within the Agent that would permit him to disprove 13's existence and shuffle him out of the deck.

Myerson had once asked his underworld leads to give him the scoop on Agent 13 and had come up dry. He concluded that the Midnight Avenger was most likely a dangerous paranoid, who must be humored.

Gyrakos, who was born in a land of ancient legends and myths and who had heard vague tales of the Brotherhood, was a sympathetic listener.

Halloran studied the man as if he were a bug under a microscope. He'd seen every type of flapper and scammer on the street before . . . but something about *this* bird was different.

It was Walters, though, who got down to business. "What do you know about the Masque?"

"Too little, save that he belongs to the Brotherhood. "

Gyrakos nodded, with the smug look of one in the know. This irritated Myerson.

"What the hell is 'the Brotherhood'?" he snapped.

"There isn't time to go into the checkered, labyrinthine history of the Brotherhood," responded Agent 13, "but it has existed since the ancient kingdom of Lemuria. In the past, it guided mankind along the paths of good. Unfortunately, as the film demonstrated, this is true no longer. Unless immediate steps are taken, time is short for civilization."

"Oh, bullhockey!" Halloran snorted. "Call the guards."

Removing a special set of gloves he wore to avoid leaving fingerprints, Agent 13 lifted up his hand. "What do you see on my palm?"

"This is ridiculous!" Halloran snarled angrily.

"Shut up, Jack." said Buckhurst coolly. "We see nothing. What is your point?"

In answer, Agent 13 reached into his vest pocket and withdrew the Seer Stone. Tossing it across to Buckhurst, he held up his palm.

"Now look at it," Agent 13 said. Buckhurst, peering through the stone, saw the number 13 and the Omega symbol—the same symbol as adorned the Masque's hood.

"This doesn't prove anything," Halloran said, sneering, "except that you're probably one of the them—"

"I *was* one of them," 13 responded coolly. "That is why they fear me and why you should listen to me. But, now, silence, for time is short. Already, the Brotherhood has tightened its fingers around Germany, Italy, Russia, and Japan. You want proof? Look at this." As he spoke, he threw photographs down on the table.

One after another, the men seated there lifted the pictures, studying them intently. There were photographs of documents, with attached translations from the German, giving figures indicating massive rearmaments. There were photos of secret U-boat factories in Sweden, blueprints of new tanks and rockets, plans for a hidden rocket base at a place called Peenemunde, photos of the training of fighter pilots in sham "Aero sports clubs," and, finally, meticulously detailed plans for global conquest.

"Is this stuff real?" spat out Gyrakos, knowing that, if it was, Hitler was in violation of every treaty Germany had ever signed. "This means war!"

"Yes," answered 13 to both questions.

"Where did you get these?" asked Myerson.

"I cannot, of course, divulge that, but if you check the figures and the locations mentioned, you'll find them correct."

"What are these?" Walters asked, pointing to another stack of photos 13 dropped on the desk.

Halloran picked them up.

There was a picture of Adolf Hitler with his high command. A picture of Mussolini in Ethiopia, a picture of Tojo aboard a Japanese carrier, a picture of Stalin in a darkened room. . . . And in each of the shots, one face was circled—that of the German officer 13 had killed in Istanbul. Always in the background, always shadowed, always slightly different, but recognizable just the same.

"His name was Colonel Reinhardt Schmidt of the SS. Until recently, this man was one of the Brotherhood's primary operatives."

"You said 'was.' Have they deactivated him?" asked Buckhurst, his scientist's voice implying neither belief nor disbelief, simply the need for information.

"No. I did," the Agent responded. "As you see, the Brotherhood now has each of these countries in its grasp. And the Hand Sinister is reaching toward the throat of America. In this nation lies mankind's last, best hope. In other countries, these criminals need only sway a few men, but here, they must sway public opinion. Hence— terrorism. We must stand united. Only with this," he said, holding up the Seer Stone, "do we have a chance of removing the cancer that has already infected the nation."

As the others watched the Agent, the clock began to chime. It was a cold, terrifying moment, and all the men went silent. When the last bell sounded, Myerson was the first to speak. "The ball's in his court."

Even through his disguise, a strange look could be seen to cross 13's face—a look of stunned realization as he saw, instantaneously and clearly, the subtlety of the Masque's plan.

"Hit the ground!" he shouted as he dove to the floor. But his understanding came too late. Before the crime fighters could move, a hail of machine-gun fire turned the penthouse windows into jagged shrapnel. . . .

Four assassins, wearing black masks and dark suits, burst through the windows into the room, spraying lead death.

Bullets hit Buckhurst from both sides, spinning his chair wildly around and dumping his body into the fireplace. Gyrakos jumped to his feet, only to be drilled to the ground by a bullet. Halloran tried to duck under the table, but a single shotgun blast shattered the wood. He looked up, stung, only to have a second blast take off his head.

Myerson tried to jump across the table to safety but was hit in the back with a shot that sent him sliding across the conference table like a giant broom, mopping up the papers and ashtrays on the way.

Walters ran for the door. A shot rang out. He slipped in a pool of Buckhurst's blood, fell to the floor, and did not get up.

Crouched in the corner of the room, Agent 13 drew a .45 and started firing his special high impact bullets. The killers leaped for the windows as his shots gouged walls and shattered timbers. Their Thompsons turned on 13. He pulled his hat over his face.

It seemed a stupid, futile gesture—the hopeless, instinctive action of a desperate man. One of the assassins even laughed as the machine guns blew 13's body about the room like a piece of litter.

Then, as quickly as the noise had come, came the silence. One of the assassins grabbed the Seer Stone from the floor where it had fallen from Buckhurst's lifeless hand. Drawing out a small spray canister, he squirted a liquid substance onto the photographs. They began to smoke and, within instants, were nothing more than gray ash. As he did this, another assassin produced a grappling hook and, stepping out the window, hurled it upward. The two other assassins warily backed to the window, firing a shot here and there into a twitching body.

There was the sound of a grappling hook striking the roof's top ledge and the soft sound of bodies padding up the side of the building.

AFTER THE ASSASSINS

Agent 13 groaned softly. His body convulsed in pain. Silver spots swam before his vision. His eardrums, numbed by the horrible cackle of the machine guns, screamed in harmony with sirens howling in the distance.

Throbbing pain told 13 that the murderous lead rounds had struck him in numerous places. What he didn't know was if his protective, bullet-proof garb had held. 13 felt the floor below him. There was no blood. The knowledge was of slight comfort as he fought off the darkness that threatened to enshroud him.

Painfully, the Agent pulled himself up, having no time to marvel at the thin material, barely heavier than wool, that had saved his life. The dumpy-looking coat and hat had stopped the slugs from ripping him to shreds.

A glance at Buckhurst's lifeless hand told 13 that the assassins had acquired an unexpected bonus—the Seer Stone. He had to get it back!

Ignoring the pain of cracked ribs and deep bruises, he softly repeated an ancient mantra he had been taught in childhood. With the repeated utterance of a single word, vibrations in the body, generated by the brain, wrapped 13 in a soothing cloud of internal consciousness. Waves of energy coursed through his body, and the pain subsided. Such was the power of the Agent's meditations.

Such was the power of the Brotherhood's teachings.

Returning to the material world, the Agent heard the insistent whine of distant sirens coming closer. Moving across the room, he quickly surveyed the massacre scene. Buckhurst lay in a twisted heap with his head in the cold fireplace. Assistant Attorney General Myerson lay across the table, his head hanging over the edge, dripping blood to the floor like a tap with a broken washer. The remains of Gyrakos, which the assassins must have used for target practice, were scattered about like so many old rags.

From somewhere in the room, though, 13 heard what he thought was a soft moan. But he could not determine which of the victims it came from. An expert at first aid, the Agent had a hard decision to make—should he save the wounded man, or pursue the assassins, who, even now, were slipping away across the rooftop? The sirens screamed louder. Long ago, 13 had become a master of hard choices.

Agent 13 was a battered sight as he jammed a new clip into his pistol, threw off the bullet-proof coat that would have hampered his dexterity, and climbed out the window to a narrow marble ledge. The shadows of the assassins could be seen swinging from one rooftop to another with the aid of their grappling hooks.

Seven stories below him, a fleet of police cars raced toward the building.

He had to get to the next rooftop. 13's eyes scanned the dirt-encrusted brick wall of the opposite building, looking for a ledge. There was none, and he cursed the lack of a grappling hook. Then, he spied a damp flag, dangling from the top of a flagpole twenty feet below him.

It was an impossible jump, of course. But Agent

13 had learned long ago that there are no impossibilities, merely improbabilities. Dashing along the ledge with a speed and dexterity usually reserved for professional gymnasts, he leaped out and down toward the flag.

For a moment of ice, he hung frozen in the air. He missed the pole, but then his hand caught the fabric of the flag. There was a sharp ripping sound as the worn fabric tore. . . .

Then it stopped. The Agent's life hung precariously by the tattered strands of Old Glory. Peering into the night, he scanned the lines of the rooftops but could see no trace of the assassins in the velvety fog.

Closing his eyes, the Agent blocked out the insistent whine of police sirens, the view of the ground still far beneath him, the sound of the strands of fabric slowly parting. His mind's energy sought one thing only—the assassins.

Using a technique he had learned from the Brotherhood, he concentrated on absorbing the energy of those he pursued into his own being. As a result, their shadowy forms appeared on his closed eyelids. Concentrating on these distant shadows, without opening his eyes, Agent 13 took careful aim. His gun let out a loud roar, and . . . in the distance, probably on the rooftop of the elegant apartment building next door . . . he heard the thud of his bullet striking a human body. He saw a sudden burst of light as the assassin's body burst into flames, and cremated itself from within. . . .

Jindas! The Brotherhood's killers! The Serpentine Assassins. Hidden in life. Burned in death.

Suddenly, the Agent was pierced by a sterile, white searchlight.

"Freeze!" an amplified voice shouted from below. Agent 13 twisted, looking down. A score of police marksmen targeted him from the open parking lot, crouching behind their cars. Without his bullet-proof jacket, he would be torn to shreds by their bullets.

"Don't shoot!" he shouted back in the projectionist's voice, dropping his gun to the pavement. "I am a government employee! The assassins are escaping!" he cried, pointing into the distance.

"No tricks, buster. Move and we'll drill ya!" returned a voice from below.

The Agent was trapped. Holding on to the flag, he peered into the gloom, cursing, as the assassins escaped. But there was no help for it. Now he had to keep up his role of the projectionist.

He remembered his training at the Shrine—how he'd been taught to hang motionless from a tree limb for over twelve hours. Those lessons had saved his life many times in the past. But he was impersonating the projectionist, who, without 13's special training, probably couldn't last more than another few moments.

Down on the street, the marksmen still held him in their sights as ambulances screamed up to the scene and attendants tumbled out with stretchers for the dead and wounded.

"Help!" 13 shouted. "Jeez! Get me off of here!"

Near the base of the flagpole, a window opened. The heads of several policemen appeared, staring upward.

"I can't hold on!" 13 babbled.

"Just take it easy, don't panic!" one cop ordered in panic-stricken tones.

The heads disappeared. Apparently someone with authority had arrived. A graying head appeared, and world-weary eyes stared up at the dangling Agent.

"How'll we get him down, sir?" one cop asked breathlessly.

"Lower the damn flag!" snarled the grizzled old captain.

Grabbing the ropes, the cops pulled and, accompanied by the squeaking of winches, they hauled in Agent 13, clinging to Old Glory.

"How the hell did you get out there?" the old captain asked.

"I dunno!" 13 stammered. "Adrenaline, maybe. Like little old ladies liftin' cars offa kids."

Suddenly, the milling, uniformed police officers in the room parted like the Dead Sea, and out stepped a man dressed in a plain gray suit and tie and a battered fedora.

"Detective LaMonica," the man said in a bored voice, flipping out a well-worn wallet, flipping it open, then flipping it shut all in a blur of movement.

One look at LaMonica, and Agent 13 knew he was nobody's fool. The man's keen, hawklike eyes surveyed the Agent.

"Cuff him," he said matter-of-factly to two nearby uniformed cops.

The officers quickly obeyed, slapping bracelets on the disguised Agent's wrists as LaMonica stepped over to the window ledge and peered up at the flagpole.

"Hey!" 13 protested. "What's with the rough stuff? I'm innocent! The guys that did this are getting away!" Standing behind LaMonica, Agent 13 began to talk rapidly, as though tense and keyed up.

"I-I was showing a film, top secret stuff, and then there was glass all over the place and flying bullets. . . ."

"Yeah?" LaMonica said noncommittally. Turning around, LaMonica eyed 13.

"You got an ID, mister, or just a mouth?" LaMonica asked.

"Of course I got an ID. But how'm I supposed to get to it?"

With a lazy gesture, LaMonica brought forward a cop, who proceeded to frisk 13 quickly and efficiently. Pulling the Agent's wallet from his pants, the cop handed it to LaMonica.

LaMonica studied an official government security card.

"Howard Richardson," he read aloud.

"That's me. Member of the union since '32," said 13.

"Union rules require you to carry a .45, do they?" LaMonica asked, holding up Agent 13's gun, wrapped in a handkerchief.

"That's Halloran's gun! I defended him with my life and—"

"Get a lot of exercise in the projection booth, do yah?" LaMonica continued conversationally.

"What? Exercise?"

"Since when does a wheezy old guy like you dash across a ledge and make a jump like that?"

"I told yah, I didn't know what I was doing. I just—"

"And I got a witness who said you fired a shot. Since when does a guy hanging for dear life from a flag got the time or the nerve to go takin' pot shots over rooftops? Plus he says you started some sort of fire—"

"I'm a veteran. Three times decorated in the Great Wa—" the Agent began indignantly as LaMonica stepped once again to the window and stared out at the street.

"Stash it," LaMonica said. Looking back, he smiled. "Walters is still alive. We'll see if he recognizes you."

Looking out the window, 13 saw a stretcher being carried from the main door of the large marble building. Unlike the others, the face of its occupant wasn't covered. Kent Walters, the National Security Advisor, had miraculously survived the carnage.

"Take 'im out," LaMonica said to two cops. "Where's Doulson?"

"Just coming out of the building now, sir," reported a cop, who was watching out the window.

"Good. Let's go."

Agent 13 was led out into the drizzle, where he stood and watched as LaMonica spoke to a fat, balding man—apparently Doulson, another detective at the scene. He'd just come down with the critically injured Walters.

"Whaddya get out of him?" asked LaMonica.

"Not much except that four men entered the room through the windows and sprayed the place."

"Professionals."

Doulson shrugged. "Sure."

"Did he get a make on them?"

"No, they wore masks. What about him?" Doulson looked at 13.

"Claims he was the projectionist. Can Walters talk?"

"Give it a try. They got him pretty doped up."

LaMonica led the way to the ambulance, which was blowing blue plumes of exhaust, waiting to vanish into the night. Two men were loading the stretcher bearing Walters inside, under close supervision of a doctor.

"Hold it a minute, boys," LaMonica said, flipping out his badge.

"This man is in extremely grave condition!" the doctor snapped.

LaMonica gave him a look that said some things were more important than a man's life right now—information being one of them. The doctor, used to cops, mumbled, "O.K., but make it quick."

"Mr. Walters, I am Detective LaMonica. This gentleman claims to be from your department. Could you identify him? It's extremely urgent."

Walters rolled his glassy eyes. "Of course," he responded in a weak voice.

LaMonica led Agent 13 to the open ambulance. The National Security Advisor's eyes cleared for a moment as he evaluated him.

Would Walters betray him? Was the man able to think clearly? Quickly, Agent 13 began to talk in his projectionist voice, hoping Walters picked up on the hint.

"Mr. Walters, I thought you'd had it!" he said breathlessly. "I chased the thugs to the roof, and took a couple of shots, but—"

"Shut up," said LaMonica, shoving the Agent forward. "Do you know this man, Mr. Walters?"

Walters looked at Agent 13 for a long moment, then said weakly. "He is . . . our projectionist."

"That's all, dectective!" said the doctor, elbowing them aside.

It took all of 13's training to keep him from exhaling a sigh of relief. As the orderlies slammed the doors of the ambulance shut, 13 turned to LaMonica, who was still regarding him with a keen look.

"There's still somethin' I don't like about you, pal. Let's say we go down to the station and have a little chat—you being a material witness and all."

"The cuffs?" 13 asked, raising his shackled hands.

"All right, uncuff him," LaMonica growled, "but keep your eyes on him," he told the uniforms who accompanied them.

Agent 13 shook his wrists to get his circulation going, smiling inwardly as LaMonica and his men headed for a squad car.

The Agent relaxed. His escape would be simple. All was going well. Walters had come through for him. He'd be after the assassins again within moments.

One of the uniforms opened the back door of the cop sedan and shoved the Agent inside. As the door was about to slam, 13 heard a shout from the distance and looked up. Something was going on, but the Agent couldn't see what. One of the cops stood between him and the action.

Then, the uniform looked down at 13, grinned, pulled out his pistol, and held it to 13's head. In doing so, he moved out of the way, letting 13 get a look at what was happening. What 13 saw sent a jolt of horror through him. As if seeing his own reflection in a mirror, the Agent saw the two cops escorting the real projectionist, who was swaying on his feet and looking slightly drowsy from the knockout gas 13 had administered before the meeting.

For what might have been the first time in centuries, LaMonica's stoic face broke into a wide grin. "Well, whaddya know. I got twin projectionists."

In all of his years of pursuing the Brotherhood, the Agent had never been caught quite so flat-footed. Cursing himself, he sank back into the seat. If he had killed the projectionist instead of simply knocking him out, this wouldn't have happened.

He could never let them take him in. Even if he told them who he really was, they'd never believe him. And after that, it would only be minutes before the Brotherhood, with its many eyes and ears, would eliminate him.

"Sergeant, cuff 'em both," said LaMonica, climbing into the squad car. "I don't know what's going on here, but we'll find out soon enough."

8

WHO STALKS THE NIGHT?

In his first battle with the Brotherhood after
escaping their grasp years ago, Agent 13 had
been cornered on a small island ferry that shut-
tled passengers from Manila to Zamboanga. The
Brotherhood's agents had closed in on him in the
boiler room. Trapped, 13 did the only thing he
could—set fire to the ship. He survived, but the
explosion set off by the fire sent the ship to the
bottom and killed seventeen innocent people.

Standing among the flotsam washed up on the
tropical shoreline, 13 felt deep sorrow . . . but no
regret. He knew that if his fight against the Invisible Empire were to fail, millions would suffer
death, or worse—live out their lives in slavery.

As a man without a country, Agent 13 had to
become a law unto himself. Thus, on that beach,
he swore to his Code of Death. This code allowed
for killing in only three circumstances:

First, when the victim was a member of the
Brotherhood. Second, when the victim was in
league with the Brotherhood. And third, when
Agent 13's life mission was threatened.

Agent 13 sighed. By threatening his mission,
these D.C. cops had signed their own death war-
rants.

As the squad car rolled past the Washington
Monument, 13 was sandwiched in the back seat
between Detective LaMonica and a massive lieu-

tenant who smelled of cologne and garlic. The real projectionist was in the other squad car. The Agent contemplated numerous escape strategies, finally settling upon one.

Using the skills of a Houdini, he noiselessly slipped his hands out of his handcuffs and activated a ring he wore on his left hand. The real projectionist wore a similiar ring, only his didn't turn into a lethal weapon.

Then, 13 rehearsed in his mind injecting LaMonica with the ring's poison, then delivering a swift and fatal jab to Cologne and Garlic.

Slipping his hands inside the dead officers' coats, he could draw both guns and dispatch the two uniforms in the front seat before they knew what hit them. He only had to wait for the police car to come to a stop at a traffic light.

A couple blocks ahead, the light turned yellow. As the squad car slowed, Agent 13 relaxed his muscles and then, like a cat, tensed them. He was ready to strike, when the driver's window shattered and he was staring at the headless body of the driver.

Razor-sharp shards of glass flew about the car, shredding the other cop in the front seat. Agent 13 was sprayed with blood.

LaMonica raised his weapon and lunged forward to fire, but the window next to him exploded. He slumped forward as Agent 13 dove for the floor. Cologne and Garlic failed to move in time, and his own blood joined the sprayed blood of others. He tried feebly to crawl out of his door. Death whistled his tune, and he was blown down the street like a leaf in the wind.

Agent 13 crouched on the floor, but screaming bullets turned the interior of the Ford into a hurricane of shrapnel. Bits of glass and lead tore the upholstery to lint and flesh to pulp. The horn began to wail as the driver's mangled corpse fell on it.

The squad car roared out of control, the dead driver's foot jammed on the accelerator.

Agent 13's only protection was the body of Detective LaMonica, which had toppled over on top of him.

Suddenly, the car slammed into something hard and came to an abrupt stop. There was the sound of breaking glass. Shoving LaMonica's bleeding body off him, Agent 13 cautiously raised his head and looked out the gaping hole that had been the windshield. He saw through the steam rising from the hood that the squad car had crashed through the display window of a meat market. Glancing out the car's back window, 13 saw the killing car screech to a halt behind them and two assassins jump out. The Agent caught the glassy glint of their eyes and confirmed his own suspicions.

Jindas.

He searched for LaMonica's gun but couldn't find it. He couldn't reach the guns in the front seat without exposing himself to the Jindas. One was already approaching the smoking wreck of the squad car while his partner covered him, ready to spray molten death on anything that moved.

The Agent slumped in his seat, playing dead as a glassy-eyed Jinda came to the window. Much to his surprise, the enemy did not study any of the bodies. He simply gave the blood-spattered interior a quick once-over, then drew a grenade from his coat.

Agent 13 had no way of knowing if the assassins were after him specifically, or whether they were simply engaged in a janitorial clean-up. As the Jinda prepared to pull the pin on the grenade, 13 made his move. Leaping across the sprawled body of LaMonica, he grabbed the door handle.

But the battered handle came off in his hand. Now the Jinda studied him directly, a sinister smile on his face as he grasped the grenade's pin.

Out of the corner of his eye, Agent 13 caught a glimpse of movement. The other Jinda was raising his gun. Agent 13 recognized it, and his heart sank. A Browning Automatic. If he did manage to make it outside the car, the BAR's bullets would rip him to shreds.

The Jinda pulled the pin. 13 had ten seconds. Everything went into slow motion as the Agent tensed to leap through the window at the Jinda.

The move would put him in the sights of the other assassin's BAR. But if he was to die, his mission unfulfilled, then he wanted to go down fighting, his hands clenched in death around the assassin's throat.

Then, from a completely new direction, 13 heard the rumbling cracks of machine-gun fire.

9

TRAIL OF TORMENT

Maggie Darr's life had always been inextricably connected to crime. She grew up on the South Side of Chicago during Prohibition. It was a wild and violent era. Her own father was shot dead right on the family's front doorstep.

Some said he had it coming to him. Maggie never really knew for sure. Even as an adult, Maggie would be jolted from bed by the remembered sounds of shots and screams.

Life was tough for a while, but when Maggie was twelve, her mother remarried. Maggie's stepfather was an Irish Alderman named McGarrity, who always seemed to have a great wad of greenbacks. Things took a turn for the better.

When she was sixteen, Maggie was sent to a private girls' prep school located between the mansions of Kenilworth and the factories of Chicago. Respected by educators, it was also a feeding ground for the young bachelors of Chicago, who cruised around it like sharks on patrol.

Jimmy Lasatti's gray-and-white convertible looked like a shark. And when he saw the tall, shapely, blonde girl coming out of class, he went into a frenzy. At first she was terse with him, appearing uninterested, as a well-brought-up young lady should. But the shark smelled blood— the blood of loneliness.

Jimmy's gambling uncle had taught him that

the longer you stay with a bet, the more likely it is to pay off. Jimmy took this philosophy into amorous relations, wooing Maggie in a dizzying, fairytale manner that made her the envy of her schoolmates. The cars, the yachts, and the parties overwhelmed the young girl, making her feel as if she had stumbled upon a golden garden in the midst of the dust bowl.

Maggie was deaf to her parents' pleas that "he might not be safe." Jimmy said he was in the export business. That was good enough for Maggie.

One night Jimmy took her to Como Inn, the finest and most romantic Italian restaurant in Chicago. After a leisurely dinner of pasta and Chianti, he popped the question, presenting her with a diamond ring. Maggie, wide-eyed, had no trouble coming up with "yes."

Several bottles of champagne later, they left Como, entwined in each other's arms. The valet brought Jimmy's DeSoto to the front. As they got in, Jimmy found a .45 shoved in his ear. A frog-voiced thug gave him driving instructions.

Whirling around to see, Maggie's fear turned to revulsion. The thug in the back seat had hideously distorted features that resembled candle drippings much more than a nose, eyes, and a mouth. Purplish skin surrounded hideously misshapen, bulging eyes and a drooping hole of a mouth that could never close all the way. His nose barely projected beyond the contours of his face, and his ears were small lumps of butter melting off a hairless scalp.

Maggie started to scream, but the thug, who she would later know as "Waxface," punched her. Revulsion turned to rage. No one had ever dared strike Maggie Darr before. She screamed and kept on screaming. The thug hit her again and kept on hitting her. Before long, Maggie was out cold.

When she came to, her wrists were cuffed together and she was hanging by the handcuffs from a hook in a meat locker, surrounded by bloody sides of beef. She had been stripped to her underwear, and her skin was blue from the cold. Her screams got attention. A large wooden door flew open and a pin-striped thug stepped through.

"Let me down!" she shrieked.

Beyond the thug, Maggie could see a man she knew from pictures in the *Daily News*—Lucky Milano. Lit by a bright, overhead light, Lucky was a dapper sight. Medium height, he wore a crisp blue suit with a flower at the lapel and was surrounded by a squad of torpedoes the Navy would be proud to own.

For the moment, Lucky wasn't paying any attention to Maggie, however. He and his boys were standing in a circle, staring at something Maggie couldn't see.

But the thug at the door walked toward Maggie. Suddenly conscious of her partial nakedness, Maggie eyed the man whose face was shadowed by his fedora. As he drew closer, she saw that it was Waxface. She gagged. His hideously contorted mouth grinned at the sight of her horror.

Suddenly, she heard a loud, pain-filled scream. Looking into the other room, Maggie could now see what was in the center of that pin-striped circle—Jimmy, tied to a chair. The cause of his hideous yell was Lucky Milano stubbing out a cigar in his eye! Maggie retched.

"I'll talk! I'll talk!" Jimmy shrieked. Maggie could then hear the low rumble of his voice and even occasionally make out words. Then there were blood-curdling, muffled shouts. . . .

Then silence. . . . And Maggie knew it was over. Despair, pain, and fear joined forces to put her mind on hold.

Some time later, a commotion brought Maggie back to reality, and she found Lucky, without a wrinkle in his pin-stripe, staring at her. She trembled like a small, trapped animal.

"Sorry, broad, but you were in the wrong place at the wrong time. Your friend Jimmy squealed big before Fats erased him. Now, toots, we gotta zap you before some tin star tips us over.

"She's all yours, Jacky," Lucky said, and his triggerman lifted his gun. "Nothin' personal," Lucky said, shrugging.

Maggie stared down the barrel of the gun. The darkness inside there would transport her to eternal darkness or to heaven or to hell. She didn't know which. But as she realized that the horror was about to end, a cooling veil fell over her. She grew calm. Many who stare eyeball to eyeball with death have known that calmness.

She would, in later weeks, remember that moment and long for it passionately.

As Jacky Red started to squeeze the trigger, Waxface spoke up. "Hey, Lucky. Remember, after I got sizzled by that acid, you said you owed me? You said that one time, just one time I could ask for something."

Maggie looked at the hideous, melted face, splotched with horrible colors, an eyeball bulging out of its dripping socket, and retched.

She knew what he was going to say, and he did. "I want her."

Maggie's heart stopped for an instant. Though the bullet in Jacky Red's gun was never fired, she died there, hanging from the meat hook.

Lucky shrugged again. "Sure thing, Waxface. But *I* get to be the first to kiss the bride."

Walking over, he put his hands on her naked torso, fondling the curves. Then Lucky kissed Maggie, cruelly, brutally.

Maggie did not spit in his face. She did not scream. She did not kiss him. She just looked at him. Stepping back, Lucky eyed her and for just a moment, his mock revelry stopped. Looking into her eyes, he saw death.

Hands bound, Maggie was thrown into the back of a limo by Waxface and a thug named Bucky Wold, a smiling guy, missing his front teeth. They drove her to Waxface's flat.

"Yer different from them others," Bucky said to Maggie as he helped haul her inside. "Usually dames yell and kick a lot when we feed 'em to Waxface."

"I won't kick until I know you'll feel it."

Once in Waxface's basement, Maggie's leg was manacled to a steam pipe. Waxface dismissed Wold, who leered at Maggie before leaving her. "I'm waiting for your kick," he mocked.

Maggie didn't say a word. She just looked back at him. Bucky shuddered and abruptly turned away. He had just stared into the grave.

Moments later, Waxface poured cologne all over himself, then walked over to stand in front of Maggie. Opening his mouth, he exposed his melted lower gums and chin bone in a hideous attempt at a smile. He only drooled.

For weeks without number, Maggie was manacled to a ten-foot-chain in Waxface's basement. The chain extended to a bathroom, a chair, and a bed, where she was the captive victim of Waxface's lechery and beatings. Days melted into nights in the living hell of the dark basement, while Maggie racked her brain for a means of escape. Finally, she figured one out.

Man has a nearly infinite capacity for self-delusion. Maggie forced herself, during each degrading assault, first, to indicate that she found some pleasure in it, then to praise him for his prowess and amatory skills.

"So your face is a bit of a mess," she'd whisper throatily. "You got a way with women any guy would envy. I'll bet I'm the first to see it."

Waxface was suspicious at first, but eventually, he began to believe her. Because he wanted to.

One night, Maggie suggested that they have a little drink to "get them in the mood." Waxface drank and drank and drank. Maggie pretended to keep up.

Almost dead drunk, Waxface dropped the bottle and reached for her. Snatching the bottle up from the floor, Maggie smashed it over the man's head as hard as she could.

It shattered. Blood mingled with rot-gut whiskey, both of them spilling down over his body. Leaping on the bed, he crawled after Maggie. As he drew closer, Maggie reached out and grabbed Waxface's lighter from a table. Flicking it, she drew a small blue flame and touched it to his whiskey-soaked clothing.

The grotesque thug burst into flames. His screams echoed off the cold, concrete walls of the basement. A ball of fire, he rolled around the floor, trying desperately to put out the flames. Instead, he spread them everywhere.

The bed caught, and Maggie, still shackled, put it out. Finally, Waxface managed to extinguish the flames. Amazingly, the man still lived. Rasping for air, he crawled toward her.

"Help me!" he gasped.

Maggie eyed the begging, pathetic face. Waxface collapsed. She didn't know whether he was alive or dead. She reached for the key chain that he wore around his neck. It was hot and burned her hand, but Maggie couldn't feel a thing. Numbly, she started to lift it off over his head.

Suddenly, Waxface's horrible face jerked up. His twisted, contorted hands reached for her throat. With a strength born of hatred, he began to squeeze Maggie's life from her body.

As blackness descended on her, Maggie's frantically searching hand clasped the broken bottle. Swinging it viciously, she jammed the razor-sharp, jagged edges straight into the man's neck.

Waxface groaned and died.

She shoved the blood-soaked dead weight off her. As she retrieved the key, Maggie felt nothing. She was numb. She turned the key in the shackle, heard a click, and watched the lock fall open.

For long moments, she just stared down at her leg. Then it sank in—she was free!

Her mind raced as she planned how to disappear. But then Maggie caught a glimpse of herself in the mirror. The face was smeared with blood and soot, black and blue with bruises, her lips split from Waxface's previous beatings.

She knew then that she had another option— she could carry out the revenge she had vowed.

Dressing in the clothes she had been wearing on that fateful night with Jimmy, Maggie went to the garage and found what she had hoped to find—a two-gallon drum of gasoline. She took it back into the house.

Spreading the incendiary fluid all over, she left the large container in the basement to explode. She pulled Waxface's wallet from his pants, took the money in it, tucked the money into her blouse, then set the flames with his ID.

The flames spread so quickly that Maggie herself barely escaped before the gas can exploded. The fire was so complete that it took the police days to identify Waxface from the charred teeth.

When Lucky heard about the fire, he only shrugged, figuring the big dolt had just gotten sloppy. He didn't spend two seconds wondering about Maggie.

He should have.

Knowing that Chicago wouldn't be safe until Lucky and his gang were dead, Maggie headed north. With part of Waxface's money, she purchased a pistol and enough bullets to learn how to use it. With the rest, she rented a lakeside cabin in Wisconsin. Here she practiced target shooting, day in and day out.

When she was good, she went hunting.

The first of Lucky's gang to see her again was Bucky Wold, the low-life scum with the toothless smile. She caught him on Oak Street.

"Bucky," she said.

He turned.

"I'm kicking."

The last thing Bucky ever saw was the flash.

Jacky Red, Lucky's triggerman, was getting a shave and a shine when the phone rang. The barber came back from the call to find the gasping Jacky gripping at his slit throat, trying to hold back the gushing blood. He might as well have been trying to stop the flow of the St. Lawrence River with a family of beavers.

The last words he heard were, "Nothin' personal."

For Fats Milligan's bachelor party, the boys rented an old speakeasy. After the movies were over, a giant cake rolled out. As Fats drooled, a curvacious woman wearing nothing but a smile popped out. For a moment, she just stood there in her birthday suit, then she disappeared back into the cake to a torrent of cat-calls. An instant later, she reappeared cradling a Thompson Model 21 machine gun. Fats froze in horror, trying to place her. She held back, watching his eyes, waiting for that split second when they flashed, "I know you." Then, she pulled the trigger, giving him and the others a one-way ticket to oblivion.

Only one name remained on her list—Lucky Milano.

Seeing his men dropping around him, Lucky began to get cautious. Being the tough that he was, he wasn't about to pack up his business interests and hoof it to New York, even though that might have been a wise move . . . considering.

Instead, he hired new bodyguards. The new thugs were heavily armed and protected Lucky well. His boys knew they could deal with any situation their boss might find himself in. Only one place worried them—that was the small neighborhood church just outside of Cicero that Lucky had attended since the day of his baptism.

Lucky liked the masses and he liked going to confession. It made him feel better, he would tell his boys. That was O.K. by them. What they disapproved of was the fact that Lucky did not allow them to enter the church with their heavy artillery. He told them it was "disrespectful."

So they would wait outside in the limos while a muscle or two, packing concealed palm heaters, entered the House of God and stood "respectfully" by the entry doors.

It was an ice-cold Saturday in April. March had come in like a lion and never left. Milano was feeling bad because the things he had to confess were piling up.

When Lucky entered the church that afternoon, he paid no attention at all to an old man in the balcony, tuning the pipe organ. Nor did he notice several old Italian women saying their penance in the back pews. He only glanced at a new priest, who had been introduced to him as Father McNulty; the good father was going about his chore of lighting the altar candles.

Lucky felt confident, knowing that his muscle was behind him in the doorway. Glancing back, he could see the thugs standing there like eagles on a rocky crag.

Lucky walked toward the enclosed confessionals in the rear of the church. There were six pine doors, side by side, recessed into the wall—two for the priests and four for the sinners. The priests would sit in the second and fifth compartments, alternately absolving the guilty first on one side, then the other. Small red lights above each of the doors informed new arrivals which of the compartments were occupied and which were free.

On the Saturdays before Easter and Christmas, the church would be packed with people wanting to confess their sins. All the lights above the doors would be lit and long lines would snake through the back of the church.

That afternoon, there were only two lights on— those above the first and second doors. The one priest on duty in the second booth was confessing someone behind the first door. Lucky walked to the third door and entered the narrow enclosure. He closed the door and knelt on the padded kneeler, awaiting his turn with the confessor.

Maggie, for her part, had tailed Lucky for weeks looking for the flaw in his protection. After several aborted attempts, she realized that the church was her only opportunity. She knew God would understand.

Noticing Lucky's fondness for the act of confession, she devised a plan. She studied the neighborhood church and its procedures, and she learned that, unless there was a holiday, only one priest would be confessing, and he always sat behind the second door.

When old Father Ponzo entered the booth that

afternoon, Maggie was the first to seek forgiveness. Kneeling in the first booth, she confessed all that she had done to Lucky's men over the last several months and why. Father Ponzo said he would have to pull major strings, but, with massive amounts of prayer, she would be forgiven.

When Maggie withdrew from the confessional, she left behind a large rock perched on the kneeler. As a result, the light above the first pine door never went off. Someone just arriving would see that the first booth was occupied and head for the third door.

Sitting in the church pew near the altar, Maggie began to recite her prayers for forgiveness. When the two old women behind her left, she sneaked back to the confessionals and quietly entered the fourth door. By not kneeling on the kneeler, she didn't activate the light outside, and no one was aware of her presence.

Turning, she faced the rear wall of the third booth and silently removed the ornamental fiber wall tiles. Then she ripped out the thick soundproofing tiles until all that separated her from the sinner in the next booth were the thin wall tiles of the third booth. These, she left undisturbed and in place.

Maggie had long ago decided that a bullet in Lucky's forehead was too kind, too quick. He had caused her months of untold suffering and humiliation. Her life had been changed forever. No, she had something special in store for Mr. Milano when he entered the third confessional.

From beneath her jacket, Maggie Darr produced a large Bowie knife with a twelve-inch hunting blade. Everything prepared, she leaned against the side wall and waited.

When Lucky arrived, he entered what appeared to be the only available confessional booth and knelt on the prayer cushion. Lucky's luck had just run out.

Maggie allowed him to say, "Bless me, Father, for I have sinned—" before she jammed the knife through the thin panel behind him. But he was leaning a little farther forward than she expected, and the knife didn't go all the way in. Impaled, he screamed and twisted as she tried to finish the job. Hearing his yells, his two sidewinders were already on their feet, pulling out their shooters as they ran to the rear of the church.

Maggie knew she had only a moment left. She didn't care about her own death, but she wanted to make sure she took that scum, Milano, with her. Thrusting her hand farther through the tile, she drove the knife deeper and watched as Lucky squirmed like an eel on a spear. Gathering all her strength, she jerked the blade sideways. The movement of the blade severed Lucky's spine. He collapsed to the floor of the booth, a lifeless mass of flesh.

Satisfied, she stepped out of the confessional, her gun before her, prepared to sell her life dearly. But, before she could fire, two shots rang out. The thugs dropped to the floor, guns sliding away from lifeless hands. Startled, Maggie whirled to face her savior.

Father McNulty!

At least, the man was dressed as a priest, but no priest Maggie ever knew carried a repeater beneath his vestments! Before she could speak, though, he spun and looked into the confessional. A flow of blood met his shoes. Lucky Milano was cutting a hard bargain with Saint Peter.

"They heard the shots outside," he said, grabbing the confused Maggie and pulling her along. "They'll be after us."

Together, they disappeared into the city.

SANCTUARY

"Father McNulty" shoved the confused Maggie Darr inside a dark gray Packard. They sped away from the church as the wail of police sirens split the air behind them.

Huddling in the front seat, staring sightlessly at the lights flashing past, Maggie Darr was in a state of numb shock. Having prepared herself for death, it was unnerving to find herself still alive.

She'd been counting on death to end this pain in her heart, she realized. Her motive for living—revenge—was gone. What was left?

The driver, this strange priest, didn't appear to have any answers. He didn't have any questions either. In fact, he ignored her and just drove.

Finally, though, after they'd apparently been driving aimlessly for thirty minutes, ducking in and out of alleys and crisscrossing the same streets, Maggie said dully, "Drop me anywhere."

"No," the priest said. "You're too hot."

Maggie shrugged and leaned back.

Soon they pulled up at a seedy-looking hotel somewhere south of the Loop.

"Oh, so this is your game, 'Father'?" Maggie said with a sneer.

The priest didn't answer. Getting out on the driver's side, he walked around to Maggie's door and opened it. When she didn't move, he reached in and dragged her out. He didn't hurt her, his touch was firm but not rough. Maggie considered putting up a fuss. One look in the man's eyes, however, changed her mind.

Why? It was a question she often asked herself later but never answered. Maybe, in that moment, her heart knew more than her brain.

The priest led her inside the hotel. The sleepy desk clerk looked up and smiled.

"Another one, Father?"

"Yes, Sam," the priest answered softly. "This poor child has agreed to give up her life of sin and follow the ways of our Lord. The usual."

"Certainly, Father," the man said respectfully, shoving over the register book. "Room 13."

Maggie craned her neck to see the signature. It read simply, "Father McNulty."

Upstairs, the priest opened the door to a room at the front. Stepping inside, Maggie saw—to her surprise—that it was clean, comfortably furnished, and more like someone's living room than a hotel room in this shabby part of town. But then, she saw the windows were barred. Crossing quickly, she found she couldn't open them.

Whirling angrily around, she found the priest watching her with a faint smile on his face. "Those are to keep people out, not keep you in." He glanced around. "The room is yours for as long as you want it, Maggie Darr."

She started. "How did you know—"

"Let's say I hear a lot in the confessional," the priest said wryly. "To continue, the room is yours for as long as you want. There're new clothes in the closet. If you're hungry, call the desk. They'll send something up."

All Maggie's suspicions returned. "Yeah? And what's the charge, 'Father'?"

"Not what you might expect." The priest's smile widened. He reached over and handed the startled Maggie the key to the room. "Leave whenever you want. But I'd suggest you at least stay the night. You could use the sleep."

He turned to go.

"Wait!" Maggie cried in confusion. "I— Who are you? Why are you doing this? I don't—"

The priest was already out the door. "Just get some sleep, kid. There's a bottle of bourbon in the drawer under the phone. If you decide to stick around, I'll see you again. If not, good luck." Giving a wry grin, he added, "And may God go with you, my daughter."

For a moment, Maggie stood, lost and alone, in the middle of the quiet room. Then, in sudden resolve, she went to the door and locked it, sliding the chain in place. He was right. She was exhausted. This place was a hell of a lot better than the dump she lived in. She could always leave in the morning.

Finding the bottle of bourbon, Maggie Darr drank a toast to life.

Maggie Darr didn't leave in the morning. She didn't leave the following morning, either. She didn't know why. The room was quiet. There were some good books lying around. The clothes fit. The food was edible. No one bothered her.

But she found herself listening to footsteps in the hall, waiting for that firm, even tread she'd been hearing in her dreams.

It came—one night. But not as she'd expected.

Maggie was half-asleep, listening to the radio reports about the growing tension in Europe when there came a knock on her door.

Her heart leaped. "Father McNulty?" she called out, her shaking hand on the chain.

"Yes, my child," came the soft voice of the priest. "I've come to see if you are well."

"Please, come in, Father!" Maggie cried eagerly, undoing the lock and flinging open the door. "I—"

She stopped, surprised at her enthusiasm. Father McNulty walked into the room, then—suddenly, without a sound—crumpled to the floor.

Maggie gasped. Closing the door, she knelt beside the priest. Then she noticed a large wet bloodstain that had been invisible on the black cloth of his robes. She was about to run for the phone, when the priest's hand closed around hers.

"No," he said. "Don't call anyone. Too dangerous. The bullet's entered between the fourth and fifth rib. You can get it out."

"Me? Are you crazy? Do I look like a damned surgeon?" Maggie demanded in anguish. "Look, you're bleeding like a stuck hog. Let me—"

"I said no," the priest said in a matter-of-fact voice. "You can do it, Maggie. You can do anything, if you have to. I'm counting on you, Maggie." His voice failed. "Maggie . . . Darr . . ."

He lost consciousness again.

Helplessly, Maggie stared at the priest. Then, she noticed something odd. His face—it was phony! Now that she looked at it closely, she could see the clever make-up job. Reaching out a trembling hand, Maggie peeled away Father McNulty. The face beneath was handsome—incredibly handsome. But, even unconscious, it was cold, cold and ruthless. Then Maggie remembered the look in the man's eyes when he'd rescued her. There had been warmth, understanding. And it was because of that look that she had stayed.

And, because of that look, she would stay—always.

Her lips pressed together firmly, Maggie picked up the phone. "Sam," she said to the man on the front desk, "I know this sounds kinda odd, but I need the sharpest kitchen knife you got—"

ASHES TO ASHES

When Agent 13 arrived at the meeting of the National Security Council earlier that night, it was Maggie who had driven him there through the dark streets of Washington, D.C. He told her to wait in the shadows for his return, keeping an eye out for anything suspicious. Unfortunately, the Jindas—expert assassins and masters of stealth—had escaped her attentive watch, as they had escaped the notice of various FBI and Secret Service agents who had also been lurking about outside.

The noise of the massacre, however, had not.

The sound of sirens filled the night by the time Maggie reached the blood-spattered meeting room. Her heart in her throat, she quickly examined the bodies, then sighed in relief. 13 was not among them.

She heard a moan and saw movement from a body. Stepping over to help him, she heard thudding shoe leather pounding up the stairs. The wounded man would have help soon enough.

Maggie fled down a fire exit, reaching the street only moments before the building was completely sealed off. Someone standing on the sidewalk beside her gave a shout and pointed upward. Maggie followed their awed gaze. High above, bathed in the police searchlight, hanging by a shredded flag, was the disguised Agent 13.

Maggie swore under her breath as the police stormed into the building. Within minutes, he was in their custody, handcuffed, and on his way to the station.

Hurrying back to her car, she waited for the squad car bearing 13 to turn the corner, then she followed at a safe distance, hoping for the Agent to make his move.

Suddenly, the tires of a black Hudson screeched around the corner, cutting her off, nearly sending her crashing into a line of parked cars. Fighting the wheel, she regained control and tore after the Hudson, sensing trouble as it closed in on the squad car.

Her instincts were good. All hell broke loose. The spitting flames of gatters began to talk. Bullets tore through metal, and the squad car swerved out of control, its driver dead.

Horrified, Maggie watched as the squad car slammed through the glass of the meat market. She saw the assassins' car pull up behind it and two men get out, one approaching the car for the "coup de grace," the other covering his pal.

Maggie reacted quickly. She didn't know whether 13 was dead or alive. It didn't matter, not now. If he was dead, she'd avenge him. If he was alive . . .

Steering with her knee, Maggie reached down and unsheathed her Thompson Model 21 submachine gun. Jamming a fresh drum-clip into its base, she roared past, firing out the window just as the Jinda was pulling the pin on the grenade.

The gunshots Agent 13 heard came from Maggie in her white roadster Lagoda, blasting away with her Thompson.

The Jinda with the grenade was struck by several bullets simultaneously. As he died, his body burst into flames. The grenade rolled from his hands into the gutter. 13 dove back into the car, throwing his hands over his head.

The second Jinda whirled, turning his armor-piercing gun on Maggie. But he wasn't quick enough. Maggie spattered him with half a dozen shots before bringing the car to a skidding stop just as the grenade went off, showering the area with deadly fragments.

Maggie instinctively ducked as the shower of metal rained down. When the smoke cleared, she turned and looked back at the second assassin, ready to finish him off if necessary. Only a pile of black ashes remained.

Suddenly, she heard the engine of the assassins' Hudson start up. A hired thug, who had been crouched down in the driver's seat of the killing car, snapped into action, sliding the car into first gear and peeling away. Maggie spun her gun around but couldn't get a clean burst off in time.

Even as the grenade exploded, Agent 13 was reaching over the front seat. Grabbing LaMonica's .38, he dove through the squad car's shattered rear window and landed on the street.

Taking careful aim, he fired a single shot. At first he thought he'd missed, but when the thug's Hudson plowed into a street lamp instead of making the turn, the Agent knew he'd hit his target.

Tossing the gun back into the squad car, he turned to Maggie, who was staring at the burning corpse of the Jinda she had shot.

"What is that thing?" she asked in disgust, looking up at 13.

"A Jinda of the Serpentine Assassins."

"What's that when it's home?"

The Agent was running over to the wrecked Hudson. "The cops'll be here any minute! Get back in the car—I'll explain later!"

Steam hissed from the Hudson's smashed radiator as the Agent flung open the car door. Out fell the gangster, a bullet hole through his neck. Pulling the corpse from the seat, 13 quickly rifled through the thug's pockets. He found the two items he needed—a blood-drenched, snakeskin wallet and the Seer Stone.

Maggie pulled the roadster up beside him as the wail of police sirens could be heard approaching from the distance. "C'mon!" she shouted.

The Agent didn't respond. He couldn't leave. Not yet.

13's concentration was focused on the corpse before him. Pulling back its eyelids, he discovered that the deceased had brown eyes. Then he touched the face. His fingers carefully moved over every inch of it, memorizing the contours, the bone structure, the skin textures, the blemishes, warts, and moles. The face of this thug was his key to the next locked door of the mystery.

Maggie fingered the Thompson again; the sirens seemed as though they were just about to scream around the street corner. But if Agent 13 was going to assume the identity of the dead man, he had to perform one last grisly chore.

Lifting the corpse by the shoulders, he dragged it to a manhole. Grabbing a crowbar from the sedan, he pried off the heavy iron cover, then slid the corpse through the gaping hole. A splash sounded as the corpse fell into the swiftly moving drainage waters. He replaced the cover, concealing the gangster's body forever in a grave beneath the capital's streets.

Maggie slid over as the Agent hurried to the car. His driving skills were exceptional. She relaxed— they'd soon be far away. Then, suddenly, they heard a loud groan. Turning around, they saw Lieutenant LaMonica crawling through the debris-strewn street from the open door of the destroyed squad car.

"How could anyone have survived that?" Maggie gasped.

"He's tough. And good," the Agent responded, easing up on the clutch of the Lagoda.

Twenty-four hours later, Police Detective Kelly LaMonica regained consciousness in room 211 of George Washington University Hospital. He was told that he was the only officer to survive the terrible massacre. When the police arrived on the scene, they had found him unconscious but wearing a unique kind of bandaging—unlike any the doctor had ever seen—which had staunched the flow of blood.

"Whoever did that saved your life, Detective," said the doctor. "You would have bled to death in the middle of the street before help arrived. Funny that whoever did it didn't stay around. You don't remember anything, do you?"

But LaMonica didn't even remember the gun battle. He proceeded to demand the official reports.

Slumped back against his pillow, LaMonica's thoughts went to the "projectionist" who shared the back seat of the squad car for those few minutes—his strange prisoner, whose body was never found.

He glanced at the report of the real projectionist. The man remembered walking into the building with the film under his arm, then nothing. The next thing he knew, "some cop" was jostling him up inside a utility closet. The lump on the man's head and a check on his background seemed to confirm the story.

While the detective was thinking about this, an orderly came into the room, bearing a bouquet of white roses. LaMonica raised his eyebrows.

"Wrong room," he said with a grin. "You must want the redhead down the corridor—"

"Not unless her name's Detective LaMonica," said the orderly, setting the flowers down on the table beside his hospital bed.

"Who're they from?" LaMonica asked, astonished.

"Dunno, there's no note. Odd number, too—thirteen. Never heard of anyone sendin' thirteen roses. Did you?"

"No," murmured LaMonica. But even as the orderly left the room and the scent of the roses sweetened the air, LaMonica remembered the rumors, the idle talk around the station, of a man who was fighting some sort of weird organization that no one else had ever heard of. . . .

One day, Agent 13 would want the favor returned.

12

TICKETS TO DOOM

The blast of a distant locomotive echoed from the darkness as the sleek, white Lagoda streaked through the streets of the warehouse district.

The Agent handled the rosewood wheel of the roadster with the finesse of a Le Mans driver. Sitting in the seat beside him, Maggie examined the contents of the snakeskin wallet.

"Guy's name was Michael Carson," she said. "You want this cash?" she asked, holding up a large wad of greenbacks.

13 gave no reply. Shrugging, Maggie stuffed the green into her pocket. "Must have been a lot more where this came from. Because this dame sure wouldn't have hung around if there wasn't."

She held up the tinted photograph of a bottle blonde with bright red lipstick, drawn-on eyebrows, and too much mascara. The Agent made a mental note of the photo.

"Hey—get a load of this. The bum had tickets to the opera!"

"Opera?"

Maggie flashed the tickets. "Wagner's *Tristan and*. . . and something. Here's a playbill about it. 'Featuring international star, China White. . . . ' "

Maggie, happening to glance at the Agent, was startled to see his face muscles tense, the color disappear and slowly return. She stared at him, but, just as she was about to make some remark, the odd look vanished. She wasn't even sure she had seen it.

As there was nothing else in the wallet, Maggie changed the subject. "Tell me about those guys back there, the ones that burst into flames."

"The Serpentine Assassins—a secret cult of ruthless killers. Some believe they come from Burma, others say Siam. Whatever the case, they style themselves as 'artists of death.' Their organization had disappeared for several hundred years until it was resurrected by the Brotherhood.

"They have a hierarchy, whose membership has multiple levels and purposes. The one you saw back there was a Jinda-Hai. That means Bat Assassin. They slip in at night and strike like bats. Jinda-Hai are the lowest in the order, completely expendable. Once the mission begins, they have a life expectancy of twelve hours."

"But why'd they burn up?"

"Before their missions, they are mesmerized through an ancient process. They lose all volition and then are made to drink *mantha*, an Eastern serum that causes their bodies to burst into flames upon death."

"How?"

"When the physical body experiences the transformation referred to as 'death,' strong chemicals are naturally released throughout the body. The combination of these chemicals and the *mantha* causes a combustible reaction that consumes the corpse and—"

She finished for him, "—leaves nothing left to identify at the scene of the crime."

"Exactly."

"Sounds like a hard way to make a living." Maggie shook her head. Then she had a sudden thought. "What about Carson? He didn't burn."

"He was the pointer."

"What do you mean?"

"A common thug who has probably never heard of the Brotherhood. He was contracted to deliver the mesmerized Jindas to their targets.

"Pointers are offered a lot for the mission because they usually don't survive to collect. If something goes wrong, they're expendable, plus—if they're caught—the pointer's past criminal record will lead the police to believe that it was a mob hit—and they won't look any further."

"And what about that weird-looking rock you took off him?"

"A Seer Stone. Perhaps the most valuable thing the Brotherhood could have hoped to find tonight. Ironically, they didn't know they had it."

"I don't follow."

"Carson took it from Buckhurst's hand on a hunch. Just a hood, unable to resist a jewel. . . . Probably figured to fence it or see if his employers might be interested. Sort of a bonus for him. He would never, of course, realize the full value of what he had accidentally stumbled across. His employers would recognize it, though."

Agent 13 fell silent. Maggie, glancing at him, sighed and settled back in her seat, watching the passing nightscape and wondering what they were getting themselves into this time.

"Isolde," said Agent 13 suddenly.

"What?" Maggie started.

"Isolde. The opera—*Tristan and Isolde*."

"Oh." Maggie shrugged and turned to look back out the window. But there was that strange expression on 13's face again. . . .

The Lagoda pulled into an abandoned alleyway, its headlights flashing on a large freight door. The Agent emerged from the car and activated the hydraulic gate. Moments later, they had parked and entered a large freight elevator.

13 operated the ordinary-looking controls that guided the device to the twelfth floor. After a pause, he took it to the fourteenth floor, and then he did something to the controls that the manufacturer had never intended, causing a special gear to kick in. The elevator slowed to a stop, then descended to another floor—a floor that wasn't supposed to be there—the thirteenth.

As a secret panel at the rear of the elevator slid open, they stepped into what appeared to be the waiting room of a corporation that had gone bankrupt in the Depression. Two couches stood against one wall. In between them was an end table adorned with copies of the *Saturday Evening Post* from 1932. In the center of the room was a tired, wooden desk. Above the desk, a calendar for the year 1934 hung from a hook next to a broken sign that read "Grogan Export." Across from the desk was a door with the words "Office of the President" stenciled on the glass.

This was, in reality, a decoy set up by 13. In the unlikely event that anyone would figure out how to work the elevator controls, all they would find as they emerged through the secret panel was this sad scene. If they persisted in being curious, anyone attempting to go through the "President" door would discover that its lock was frozen, the glass was unbreakable, and the door was unbelievably difficult to force.

The only entrance to Agent 13's sanctum was gained by swinging open what appeared to be a plain, ordinary cement pillar. Agent 13 did this and stepped into the darkness beyond.

13 flicked on the light, automatically scanning the room to make certain all was as it should be.

Though it was only one of the Agent's many secret lairs, the Washington sanctum was a complete crime-fighting headquarters. A target range extended the full length of the room. The wall on one side of the range was filled with weapons ranging from automatic rifles to swords to blow-guns. The wall opposite held a small but amazingly comprehensive library.

Beyond the rows of books, barely visible from the secret door, was a clutter of machinery. The blade of an autogyro jutted out of the shadows. Next to it was a diving suit complete with shiny brass helmet. Beyond that was a small but well-outfitted chemistry lab and a great oak table laden with books, maps, charts, and a huge globe.

Of particular significance was a large wall map on which 13 had traced several circles. For years, he had been searching for the fabled Shrine—the place where he'd been taken blind-folded as a child. The place from which, as a young man, he'd been cast out to die after he'd discovered their heinous secrets. The secret place that was the heart of the Brotherhood.

Below the map was a small gymnasium and, opposite it, Agent 13's disguise atelier.

Tables filled with make-up lined the walls. Hundreds of wigs perched upon faceless heads. Racks and racks of clothing stood in the center of the room. The ghosts of hundreds of people lived— ghosts that Agent 13 invested with life.

Maggie, entering beside 13, looked at him to say something but saw the Agent's eyelids flutter. Instantly, she reached into her purse and drew her revolver. Something was wrong.

Without warning, the room turned into a combat zone. Crackling explosions hammered at their ears. Shrieking missiles streaked about in wild, unpredictable patterns.

Half-blinded by the bursting light, Agent 13 and his beautiful counterpart hit the floor.

Shielding her eyes from the fiery brilliance, Maggie scanned the room, looking for the source of the attack. Raising her gun, she was about to see if she could smoke anything out when Agent 13 knocked the gun from her hand.

Standing up, he stepped into the barrage, ignoring Maggie's scream of alarm. The streaking projectiles bounced off him like Ping-Pong balls.

"Fireworks!" Maggie muttered, disgusted.

Though generally soft spoken, the Agent could command a bellowing voice. "Ray!" he shouted over the barrage.

A figure loomed beside Maggie, reaching for her gun. Instinctively, she spun and threw a lethal Savate kick at it. A hand of steel caught her foot in mid-air, nearly sending her toppling over.

"Maggie, meet Ray Furnow," 13 said.

Holding her foot, snickering, was a man of Asian extraction, whose age might have been anywhere from twenty to sixty. He grinned at her with a slightly stupid expression that was belied by cold, calculating eyes.

"You said he was dead," Maggie said, jerking her foot away. "Killed in a knife fight in Bangkok."

"I thought he was," the Agent responded.

"Foolja agin, podner," Ray said, smiling, in the voice of a cowpoke. Then, in his best bad Charlie Chan, "Number Nine Wife chase me down. Had to take powder before forced to drink powder."

Agent 13 stepped over to Ray and examined a small pellet the Oriental held in his right hand.

"I call it 'Fourth of July in a Marble,' " Ray said.

"The propellant?" Agent 13 asked.

Ray grinned. "You maybe forget about that so minor incident in Saigon?"

"Maybe." 13 sounded noncommittal.

Ray shrugged. "Cobalt, C-140, dragon's tooth, and ginseng."

"Ginseng? That's real scientific," Maggie said sarcastically.

"Keeps it in air longer," Ray said. Producing a ring, he held it up. "I've put disk into ring you wear on your finger. Use if problem occur."

13 peered at the ring. A small Chinese coin was mounted in the center. Ray pointed to a tiny raised edge. "Push here and the fireworks begin."

"I already wear a ring, sometimes two," the Agent said.

Ray looked at him, puzzled for a moment. Then he grinned in understanding, making the motion of burning a number onto someone's forehead.

"I will make it into cuff links."

13 smiled a rare smile as he pocketed the ring anyway. When his hand came out of the pocket, it was holding the Seer Stone.

"I need a copy. Can one be made from glass?" 13 asked, handing the stone to Ray.

The Oriental pulled a loupe from his pocket and studied the stone with an expert eye. "Have never seen jewel like this. How soon you need?"

"Tomorrow."

Ray breathed a sigh of relief. "Tonight problem, tomorrow no problem."

Maggie eyed the little man. Something about him didn't play real. Something? *Nothing* about him played real!

"Nothing about me *is* real," Ray responded.

She looked up with a start. "You didn't tell me he could read minds!" Maggie said accusingly to the Agent.

13 didn't answer—he was walking to the atelier. Ray and Maggie followed. Glancing at Maggie, Furnow smiled.

"When man is trying to keep away from fifteen wives and ninety-four children, man must not only read minds but have a sixth sense," he said.

Then, gesturing toward 13, he added, "Tell me about the case that furrows his brow."

"An American scientist with a horrible new weapon, a burning dirigible, an exploding train, a building blowing up, a man with a mask making an ultimatum, a clock striking midnight, and a room full of dead lawmen. How does that sound?" Maggie said glibly.

"America in grave danger," Ray Furnow pronounced.

"Brilliant deduction," Maggie snapped. "Why would someone go to all that trouble to threaten America?"

"Maybe person *wants* America," Ray said, then shrugged again. "Although, if I wanted to take over America, I would just shoot President."

Sitting down in a chair before a table filled with supplies, the Agent muttered, "Ray's psychic abilities are matched only by his ignorance and lack of common sense."

"So I gathered from the wives and kids." Maggie laughed.

"What is the matter with that plan?" Ray asked.

Maggie took the bait. "Because you'd have to shoot the Vice President, too."

"So, I kill him, too. Then who takes over?"

"Whoever's next in line. I forget. Speaker of the House, maybe. Or else the President Pro Tem of the Senate, Secretary of State, National Security Advisor. . . . I don't know." Maggie shrugged.

Ray yawned. "A lot of killing. Most boring. Maybe I would find another way. What if I—"

While Maggie and Ray discussed ways to take over America, Agent 13 calculated his plan of attack. 13's only link to the Brotherhood's plot was Carson's opera tickets for the following evening at the Met. The dead Carson didn't seem like the type to be interested in Wagner unless he had a reason . . . like payment.

And there was something else, another reason for 13 to attend the opera . . . a reason more personal than he would care to admit.

13 drove the memories from his mind.

He had a night and a day to perfect their disguises. He had to concentrate, he had to be exact, for the slightest deviation could spell death for all of them.

Lost in concentration, the agent stared up at the "faces" of past disguises that looked down at him from upper shelves—a silent audience. Near him, large boxes overflowed with eyelashes, false beards, mustaches, and hair pieces of all colors and textures. Jars containing warts, moles, and even birthmarks sat like goods at the market.

Looking into the mirror, the Agent began peeling away his disguise of the projectionist. For just a brief moment—not noticed by either Maggie or Ray Furnow, who were disputing constitutional questions—the real face of Agent 13 could be seen. It was that of a surprisingly handsome man in his late thirties with intense, light eyes.

Staring into the mirror, the Agent silently plotted his disguise strategy.

He must build "bones" to match the cheek bones of the man he had killed. Then he would apply a layer of wrinkled latex—a second skin used to simulate the flesh of others. Finally, he would match the facial hair and the pigmentation, all reproducing the vivid image his mind retained from his brief study of the dead thug.

Tomorrow night, the Agent's face would be gone, and the face of a dead man would come back to life. And, after that, he would transform Maggie into the blonde floozy whose picture Carson carried so proudly.

THE SIREN'S SCREAM

A jagged streak of lighting flashed through the darkness of New York's skyline, lighting the opera house as if the gods were taking photographs. Below the brooding structure, late patrons stepped quickly from limousines, racing up the steps of the Met as servants hurried to keep pace with large umbrellas, protecting their employers from the driving rain.

Inside the ornate structure, the well-dressed men and women were led to their seats. Presenting his tickets to an usher, Carson and his blonde girlfriend, Crystal Murdow, were taken to an exclusive box that afforded an excellent view of both the stage and the audience.

Both acting their roles, Agent 13 as Carson appeared highly uncomfortable in his obviously rented tuxedo, while Maggie—in a sequined, low-cut gown and a garishly colored feather boa—accepted the disapproving stares of the women with gum-smacking aplomb.

"Geez, Mickie, it looks like a flower bed, don't it? See, the ladies in their fancy dresses are the flowers and you men are the dirt? Get it, Mickie? The dirt!" She laughed raucously as Carson regarded her with pride and admiration.

But Maggie's laughter was forced, all part of the act. For Maggie knew that somewhere in this gaily appointed room was a deep evil. Somewhere was a force that had wrought disaster after disaster. Where would it strike next?

Maggie felt naked and exposed in the elegant box seat. Anyone in the opera house could pick them off. Holding tightly to Carson's arm, Maggie played his woman for all it was worth. It was a role she enjoyed. But Maggie knew that the admiring smile the Agent beamed upon her was not for her eyes but for whatever unseen eyes were observing them.

"Mr. Carson?" a voice said suddenly.

Maggie started, whirling in alarm. Standing behind them was an usher holding a tray.

"Yeah?" Carson replied coolly.

The usher held the tray out. Resting in the middle was a large envelope with the name—Mickie Carson—written on it. Languidly, 13 lifted it from the tray.

"Uh, hey, wait a half a sec, pal," he said as the usher started to leave.

"Sir?" the usher replied, turning and looking down his nose.

"I got a letter to deliver to the person who gave you this envelope."

"I'm sorry, sir, but I'm afraid I don't know where it came from. The central office asked me to deliver it, and they're now closed."

"Don't worry. Just take the note, they'll find you." The Agent slapped a sealed envelope into the usher's hand, along with a twenty dollar bill.

"Whatever you wish, sir," the usher replied as he left, with double his night's usual wages.

Carson turned to Crystal. "Honey, flash around that rock I gave ya."

"You know I'm not dat kinda girl. Do I got to?" Maggie cooed, smacking her gum.

"Do it for me, babe."

The disguised Maggie relented, lifting the Seer

Stone from between her breasts where it hung from a golden chain. Then, like a B-girl showing off a new gift, she flashed it about for all— particularly those unseen eyes—to see.

This was the bait. In the letter 13 gave to the usher, he explained how he—Carson—had taken the strange jewel from the dead Buckhurst's hand. It looked valuable. He was interested in selling it, if the price was right. He knew some other fences who would be interested in it, of course, but he was an honorable guy. He always believed in giving first right to his employer.

The theater lights dimmed and darkness curtained the opera house in a shroud that felt sinister to 13 and Maggie.

The prelude to Wagner's *Tristan and Isolde* softly wooed the great hall in an emotional yearning, a tenderness, and an unrestrained outpouring of love's declaration. Agent 13, whose life was devoid of the form of sentimentality that such music brings, could only marvel at the mathematical symmetry of the sound—the balance of notes against notes, of instruments against instruments, the soft, mournful sigh of the violin with the dark foreshadowing of the drums, the expectant horns and the brooding oboes.

As the music played, Agent 13 tried to make order out of the strange and twisted plot being played out by the Hand Sinister. A Zeppelin in flames, a train tumbling over a bridge, an aircraft factory exploding, and, finally, Dr. Fischer. How were they related and how did the Masque fit into it all? What did this impossible ultimatum have to do with it? Where would the hand of death strike next?

As Wagner first lulled him and then bombarded him, 13 suddenly realized that the answer was all around him.

Isolated from the rest of the symphony, the music of any individual instrument can be flat, meaningless. But in concert with the other instruments, it becomes an integral part of a moving story painted upon a vast and beautiful canvas.

Likewise, any single crime of the Brotherhood's was in itself meaningless. But 13 knew that the Hand Sinister built his plots upon repeating themes to be played by a vast array of instruments. Each operative's part was small. Each plot was built upon another, all moving toward a grand finale.

The Masque was the conductor of the Hand Sinister's composition. The Masque's ultimatum was the overture. It was up to the Agent to figure it out before the crescendo of doom thundered the voices of mankind to silence. Within the Masque's seemingly unrelated crimes was a melody that bound them together—a repeating theme that should give him the clue to the conclusion.

13 was jolted back to the real orchestra as the curtain parted. The music of the instruments slowly gave way to a chorus of voices, and then a single voice rose above them, its purity and sweetness suddenly commanding the opera house.

Almost unconsciously, Agent 13 sat forward in his seat, his wandering attention captured.

Maggie Darr's attention was captured, too—by 13's strange reaction. Raising her opera glasses, Maggie looked at the woman. She was Isolde . . . and she was striking. Even beneath Isolde's blonde wig, the woman's dark beauty smoldered like a flame, the somber medieval-style gown floated about her like smoke.

Maggie glanced at the program. Of course, China White. Maggie's eyes went once more to Agent 13. His attention was completely riveted upon the woman. Maggie suddenly remembered

13's odd reaction to the name in the car.

"She is stunning!" Maggie whispered to her companion. He made no response. His heart and soul were, it seemed, wrapped up in that beautiful figure upon the stage. Seeing his face—and knowing that the expression on it was *his* expression—not Mickie Carson's—a pit opened in Maggie's stomach and all her hopes and fears seemed to drop into it.

Agent 13 was in a world of another place in another time:

Moonlight in a scented garden.

She floated, dreamlike, above the glowing sand.
His heart pounded, ached.

Against hers.
Pounding.

Gardenia and night jasmine tickled the air
As he drifted into the abyss of her eyes.

And he might have disappeared forever had it not been for—

Suddenly aware of another presence in the opera box, Agent 13 crashed out of his trance and whirled around, prepared to strike. But it was only the usher again, holding a silver tray.

The usher was apologetic for having startled him. "Excuse me, sir. I am so sorry to have disturbed you. I have been asked to deliver these."

Agent 13 carefully lifted two items from the tray. One was a boutonniere consisting of an ivory-white rose surrounded by delicate silver lace, the other was heavy linen notepaper of the same color. Tearing it open, Agent 13 found a printed invitation to attend a "private party" that night at the Brown Rat. A single phrase was scrawled at the bottom—"After the performance."

They were biting.

14

BELOW
THE BROWN RAT

Shortly after the end of World War I, a group of self-appointed guardians of public morals bonded together to pass the Prohibition Act. For almost fourteen years, the unpopular and unenforceable law remained on the books, producing more organized crime than sobriety. Finally, in 1933, it was repealed by the 21st Amendment. But the damage had been done—cities were catacombed with illegal speakeasies, and a nearly indestructible system of organized crime controlled large segments of American life.

The legalization of alcohol was bad news for the crime bosses. Now, instead of having to simply pay off the cops, they had to compete with legitimate businessmen. Strong-arm tactics, protection rackets, arson, and knee-cappings were enough to take care of these minor annoyances, but what was to be done with the real estate and the underground apparatus that had kept the mob going for so long?

Thus, the innocently naughty speakeasies turned into opium dens, smuggling warehouses, slaving docks, and brothels. And some, like the Brown Rat, were all of the above.

A dark, dockside joint near Chinatown, the Brown Rat was an open secret among the police, celebrities, and politicos of New York City. Cops knew better than to bust the place unexpectedly because they might come face to face with their bosses. Therefore, when it was necessary to appear to be cracking down on the Brown Rat, the police would stage a carefully choreographed raid on the establishment, string up a petty crook and a couple of illegals, and shut the place down for good measure.

The papers ate it up, the public slept easier at night, and two weeks later, the Brown Rat would open up with a new paint job and stage show.

13 thought about this as the sedan plowed through the rain-drenched streets. Capably driven by Ray Furnow, 13's assistant, the car wound its way from the Metropolitan Opera House among the back streets and alleyways of Chinatown. Still acting their parts, 13 and Maggie sat together in the back seat. They had been going over their plans, but, since the Agent was uncertain what to expect, there wasn't much they could discuss. So, they sat back and listened to Ray Furnow.

Ray's complaints practically drowned out the hum of the rented DeSoto limo he was driving.

"Wives all over the place—like fire-breathing dragons! Find another chauffeur, friend," Ray had said at first.

But 13 insisted on bringing him along.

The Agent knew the value of having a well-connected Oriental like Ray with them. If there was trouble, and they had to take refuge in the neighborhood, Ray could help open the doors of the suspicious, close-knit society.

Patiently, 13 had explained all this earlier to Ray, who shook his head adamantly.

"No, forget. I hear the patter of too many little feet."

After a moment, 13 said, "Uh, Ray, about that incident in Singapore—"

"What time do I bring the car around, boss?"

As for Maggie, it was logical for Carson to take Crystal with him to a party. She looked like a fun-loving girl in the photograph they'd found in Carson's wallet, to say nothing of the fact that Carson probably enjoyed showing her off. Beyond "Carson's" reasons, 13 appreciated Maggie's keen mind and her ability to uncover information. He also welcomed the added firepower of Maggie's gun. If things got sticky, he could depend on her. They made a good team.

Posing as Carson's driver, Ray pulled the DeSoto into the Brown Rat's parking lot, which was jammed with cars and waiting drivers. The expensive limos attested to the fact that the night's party was a big do.

"Out of the pan and into the steamer," Maggie mumbled as a valet opened her car door and helped her out.

"If we're not back in one hour, leave," 13 muttered to Ray as he climbed from the car.

The white rose attached to his lapel, the disguised Agent 13, with Maggie clinging to his arm, stepped into the elegant Chinese restaurant. Patrons could be seen dining romantically in front of large windows that overlooked the river. The lights of New York's skyline reflected off the waters like millions of heavenly stars, while large freighters slowly plied the river, bound for distant, exotic ports.

"Two for dinner?" inquired the maitre 'd' in a welcoming tone.

"We're here for the party," responded 13 in his best Big-Man-about-Town tones, while Maggie broke out her compact, making final make-up adjustments.

"Party?" asked the maitre 'd' vaguely.

13 passed the man his invitation. One look at

the card told the maitre 'd' that the low-life before him was legit.

"Your name?" He sounded faintly disgusted.

"Carson, Michael Carson."

Maggie, pouting, nudged him in the ribs.

"Oh, and this is my friend, Crystal Murdow," Carson said nonchalantly.

"How yah doin'?" she cooed, holding out her hand to be kissed.

The maitre 'd' ignored her hand, quickly turned, and summoned a nearby waiter with a snap of his fingers.

"Mr. Chen, please take Mr. Carson and his— uh—companion to table 12B."

"Please follow me." The Oriental waiter led them past several rows of round tables and candlelit booths, occupied by various members of the elite elite and the shady elite.

Expecting glitter and noisemakers, Maggie was startled when the waiter led them through a small doorway into a smaller room. Here he gestured to a quiet, lonely booth.

"Some party," Crystal whined to Mickie Carson as she took her seat.

"It'll be O.K., babe," Mickie said with crude, bluff confidence, though it was obvious to the waiter that the hood was just as nonplussed as his girlfriend.

"Enjoy yourselves," Mr. Chen said, bowing and leaving the room.

Left alone, the two sat in silence for a moment, lost in their own thoughts. Then Maggie Darr turned to Agent 13. "Tell me, who is—"

13 shook his head. "I'll tell you later what you need to know about China White."

Maggie gasped. "You read my mind!"

"It was not as mystical as you presume. I've been watching you. Your hand brushed across your heart, telling me that you were thinking of amorous affairs. You opened your mouth to speak, but, an instant later, your hand brushed across your lips, symbolically shutting them. This, added to your obvious curiosity at the opera house—"

"Curiosity! I didn't ask you a word in the opera house!" Maggie whispered defensively. Then she realized that his attention had gone to a Japanese print hanging on the wall across from the booth.

"We're being watched!" he said to Maggie softly.

Maggie followed his gaze in time to see a shadowy shape pass behind the print.

"It's a screen," 13 began, when, suddenly, the table between them began to hum and rise! Instinctively, Maggie grabbed for her purse containing her pistol, only to feel Agent 13's hand closing over her own. Then she realized that the booth was, in fact, a cleverly disguised elevator. The table wasn't rising, they were descending!

The moisture in the air and the massive, steel-plated walls told 13 that they were going down beneath river level, probably into one of the deep channels.

After several seconds, the booth slowed to a stop. Large doors carved with elaborate Chinese characters faced them on one side. The doors parted, revealing the most exotic Persian cabaret in the Western world.

The room was thick with the stench of palpable evil. The smell of burning hemp greeted their nostrils, as the wild wails of swing music stung their ears. Half-dressed "harem girls" swooned about a large stage, while gold-digging floozies seduced their men at surrounding tables, always with an eye to their next sugarpops.

"Isn't that Senator Fra—" Maggie whispered,

but the Agent silenced her with a look.

"Don't use names in here," he said coolly.

Behind them, a laughing couple stepped into the ingenious elevator they had just left. The ornate doors closed, carrying them back to the street-level restaurant above.

A large man with a pencil-thin mustache approached.

"Your names?"

"Michael Carson and Crystal Murdow."

Maggie smiled as the man checked a clipboard with a long list of names.

"Very good, Mr. Carson." he replied.

13 and Maggie started to enter the room, when suddenly the mustached man reached out and stopped him. "We ask that you check in any firearms you or the lady might be carrying." He pointed to a small room that looked like a police armory. "We provide the protection here."

"No problem." 13 didn't want trouble. He had other forms of protection, equally as deadly.

"Ooooh, imagine me packin' a rod, Mickie?" Crystal giggled with a cute little shiver.

"Gives me the chills, babe." Carson laughed. But 13 grinned as he followed Maggie to the gun checkroom. He knew that she wasn't about to part with her pistol. Ever since the days of Lucky and his gang, the pistol had become a part of her.

13 gave his .45 to the man behind the counter and was given a claim check for its return. He could feel the eyes of the mustached man watching his every move. As he went back out into the crowded room, 13 noticed that there seemed to be a lot of eyes watching the newcomers. One man especially was looking intently at the white rose on 13's lapel. He gestured to a buxom, long-legged tobacco girl, who was wearing nothing but a signboard that advertised Pyramid cigarettes.

"If we're separated, you know what to do?" 13 said softly to Maggie.

"Sure, babe," she said, grinning at him.

The cigarette girl swayed across the room on her high heels, coming to a stop in front of Agent 13. "Mister Carson, would you follow me, please?"

"Anywhere you wanna go, sugar!" Carson leered.

"Mickie!" squealed Crystal, grabbing Carson by the jacket.

The cigarette girl smiled at the gangster's blonde bit of fluff. "Not you, I'm afraid, honey. Don't worry, I'll take real good care of your boyfriend."

"And I'll take real good care of your eyes, you little—" Crystal started forward, her painted red nails glistening. Carson caught hold of her.

"I gotta do some business, Crystal baby. Here's a fiver," he said, pressing a bill into her hands. "Grab yourself some hooch. Daddy'll be back before you see the bottom of two glasses." Turning, he followed the woman's naked back through the glittering crowd.

Not breaking character, Maggie rolled her eyes, sucked in her cheeks in a pout and then flounced off toward the bar. She was stopped halfway across the room by a pair of hands closing over her shoulders. Turning, she saw a tall thug in an ill-fitting tuxedo and with a black patch over one eye.

"Watch your meat hooks," she said, shrugging his hands off her shoulders.

"Carson's fluff's got some spit. I like that!" he said, turning to a pair of the strangest-looking torpedoes Maggie'd ever seen. They were dressed like characters out of Sinbad the Sailor with colorful silk suits, huge jeweled turbans, and scimitars at their waists. But it wasn't so much their costumes that startled Maggie—it was the weird look in their eyes. They stared straight ahead, seemingly completely oblivious to what was going on around them.

The thug in the tux, meanwhile, eyed Maggie. "My hands go where they want to go, sister, and no one stops them," he said, allowing his fingers, as if by accident, to brush across her breasts.

For a moment, Maggie was back in Waxface's room. Disgust and rage overwhelmed her, nearly making her choke. She came to herself to find her hand actually opening her purse for her pistol. This was no time to make a scene. In fact, this was just what she'd been hoping to be able to run across—some hood who might have some information.

And so, instead of pulling out her gun and shooting the fellow down on the spot, Maggie Darr smiled up at him and fluttered her mascaraed eyelashes.

"Oooooh, so strong!" she cooed.

The hood tumbled.

"Say, since your buddy's takin' off, why don't we talk for a moment?"

Maggie glanced over to see Agent 13, led by the cigarette girl, vanish into the liquid crowd that swirled around and finally engulfed him. "Sure," she said coyly. "What'cha wanna talk about?"

His greasy face, cigar breath, and sweaty, meaty hands drew close to her. A wave of revulsion washed over her, followed by the strong desire for her Thompson submachine gun.

"Whaddaya say we talk about a drink, you and me," the thug said.

DARK GREETINGS

13 watched as the cigarette girl shut the heavy door behind them, abruptly silencing the music and chatter from the party room. Carefully locking the door, the girl moved forward again, walking straight toward a blank wall. Pushing on the molding, she stepped aside as the wall swung open, revealing a stairwell on the other side.

A ruse within a ruse, thought 13 as he followed the girl down the clanging iron steps. A distinct odor of water reminded 13 that they were below the river. Looking at the steel-plate walls, 13 envisioned the massive pressure of water these walls had been designed to hold back. It was an ideal hideout, safe from prying eyes and ears.

Quickly, 13 planned what he would say when he met the person who snapped at his bait of the Seer Stone. He knew it would be a member of the Brotherhood, but who? A name came to mind. How would he react when they were face to face? Just seeing her from a distance tonight, looking even more beautiful than she had looked when—

Coldly, 13 put those memories out of his mind. He forced himself to concentrate on her as she existed now, not in the twilight of their past. Was she involved with the Masque? Was she herself the Masque?

If it was China waiting below, would she be likely to know Carson? 13 figured not. Carson was a pointer, nothing more. If he hadn't just happened to pick up the Seer Stone, he would probably have been either paid off by now—or dead. Probably no one in the upper echelons of the Brotherhood had ever seen the hood face to face.

They would only know Michael Carson by his mission, which the disguised Agent felt comfortable handling. They probably wouldn't even notice any change in the Agent's voice. Fluent in twenty-six langauges, including Sanskrit, Agent 13 was also a master of speech and voice control, including ventriloquism. He could imitate anyone's voice perfectly—once he'd heard it. Unfortunately, Carson had been beyond speech when they'd met.

At the bottom of the staircase, the girl opened a large set of sealed, inlaid doors and gestured for him to enter. He immediately noticed a flickering light that seemed to dance out of the chamber beyond.

As 13 stepped through the doorway, he was bathed in a shimmering green light. The shivering cigarette girl closed the door behind him, leaving him alone, or so he thought.

Two walls of the enormous room were constructed of thick, fourteen-foot-high, plate-glass windows bound by reinforced bands of copper. Their banded construction and reinforced steel held back the massive sea on the other side, while permitting an unobstructed look at the underwater kingdom.

Large, submerged lights illuminated the plankton that filled the waters and covered the pylons supporting the Brown Rat. It was the plankton, an abundant micro-organism, that gave the underwater light its greenish hue. The almost invisible growth at the base of the ocean food chain thrived in the artificial light and drew in the larger creatures that feasted on it.

The final receiver in the late-night food chain was the great white shark, whose never-ending appetite was often rewarded by the smaller feeder fish hovering about the plankton. One of the great sharks was there now, gulping down its prey, its skin glowing green in the weird light. Agent 13 found its presence symbolic and amusing.

The room's furnishings consisted of a pair of high-backed, black, lacquered chairs and large black marble desk. The severe pieces were massive and cold. To the left of the desk, two sealed doorways led through an iron plate wall. A large mirror with a golden frame hung in the center of the metallic wall—the only touch of humanity in the otherwise spartan chamber.

The sea was the real focus of the room, the sea with its constant movement, turmoil, and never-ending life or death struggle for survival. . . .

"Welcome, Mr. Carson," said a woman's voice.

13 turned, remembering—as Carson—to give a start of surprise. In reality, 13 was surprised. Even with his acute sense of hearing, he had not heard the woman arrive, which made him suspect that the voice belonged to the one person he knew to be equally well-trained in the arts of silence and stealth. Looking in the direction from which the voice had come, he saw—framed by the graceful wings of a stingray drifting in the water behind her—China White.

Though she was now simply if elegantly dressed, her appearance was no less dramatic than it had been on the Wagnerian stage. The undulating lines of the green light's reflection in the water caressed her high cheekbones, her deep blue eyes glowed like a cat's, and the gleam of her perfect teeth slashed through the darkness like a knife in the sunlight.

"Jesus, yah scared me half to death. How'd ya get in here?" Carson asked.

"I'll ask the questions," China replied flatly.

"However you wanna do it, sugar."

Although 13 had never met Carson in life, he knew the type—a rude, cocky tough, who wouldn't take any lip from "some dame." Carson would believe he was the man in control.

13 knew the truth, however—China White was deadly. Trained by the Brotherhood in the arts of seduction, she was like a spider enticing the powerful into her web of lust and deceit, then devouring them whole. Watching her as she contemplated Carson, 13 could see her considering how best to handle this imbecile. And his mind went back. . . .

A moonlit night at the Shrine. Two young people in love. Thrust together by the Brotherhood's sinister forces, they were to view each other as lessons, objects in a grand plot so twisted that neither could understand. Love was never supposed to have happened. But something went wrong . . .

China drew near him. "I understand that you have something of ours you wish to return."

"No, no, babe. You misunderstand. *I* have something of *mine* I might consider *selling*."

"I see."

"So let's talk price."

"Let's."

"Now, the way I figure, with the market for stones the way it is. . . ."

A low sinister chuckle slowly echoed from the area near the desk. A blinding bank of arc lamps switched on. Everything whited out. It was as if someone had torn off the roof and dropped the blaring noonday sun inside.

"What's goin' on here!"

Shielding his eyes from the glaring lamps, the

Agent instantly became aware of the cold pressure of a gun barrel at his back.

"What's this?" he snarled. "What's with the big lights and gat in my back? Call off the wiper or the deal's off!"

"But you wanted to talk price, Mr. Carson. Let's start with your life. What is it worth?"

"Less than yours when I get outta here, sister!" Carson sneered.

"*If* you get out of here, Mr. Carson. . . . *If.*"

13 had expected this. The pure tone in China's voice was one of disdain.

"Now, let's start at the beginning. Please give me a full account of last night's activities."

"You're not gettin' nothin', you little bit—"

A sharp blow to his kidneys doubled 13 over. As he fell, he caught a glimpse of the hard butt of a pistol swooping down before a jagged bolt of pain shot through his neck.

"You must learn some manners, Mr. Carson." China's cool, beautiful voice was the last thing 13 heard as he slipped into unconsciousness.

The next thing the Agent knew, he was on his knees, staring at the rug. He tried to open his eyes, but all he could see were bright flashes of throbbing pain. All he could hear was the sound of heavy breathing somewhere above him.

13's arms were pulled out from under him, slamming his head against the floor. He tried to move his arms, but they were held fast by a strong pair of hands. Then he felt cold metal on his wrists, heard a click and a snap, and realized he had been handcuffed. Anstett 32 Police Restrainers, from the feel. They would be no match for his talents once he regained his strength and bearings. He looked around the room. It was then that he got his first clear look at China's assistant.

The man was a giant, towering well over nine

feet tall. Carson was appalled at the sight, but 13 was only slightly surprised. For he had seen these enormous creatures before, back in his days with the Brotherhood.

The giant was a member of a nearly extinct race called the Nephilim, or the Sons of Anak, as referred to in the Book of Genesis. They were the result of a genetic breeding experiment conducted by the Brotherhood after the reign of the Lemurians, thousands of years ago.

With the fall of the mighty Lemurian culture, civilization in the known world collapsed, and anarchy prevailed.

The Brotherhood sought a quick way to unify the world once again. Thus they created the Nephilim, men of undisputed power and strength. So impressed were the pagans that soon the giants of Nephilim were worshiped as gods.

Forming their own communities, the Nephilim flourished, while always remaining in the service of the Brotherhood. But, unfortunately, because they were different, the Nephilim made convenient scapegoats. Everything from plagues to earthquakes were blamed on them, and soon the people who had at one time worshiped these peaceful creatures began to attack them.

The Nephilim fought valiantly under the leadership of Og, the last of the great kings of Bashan. But it was to no avail, for even though they were superior in strength, they were greatly outnumbered. On the run, they fled to the only safe haven they knew—the Shrine of the Brotherhood.

During their flight, they were hunted across two continents. Many were taken prisoner. Turned into slaves, they were pressed into guard duties in palaces from Luxor to Memnon. Their children were thrown into armies where they once again distinguished themselves as great warriors and leaders.

There was Goliath, the champion of the Philistines, who was slain by David; Gabbaras, who was captured after a heated battle and brought in shackles to Rome after Emperor Claudius's Arabian victories; Idusio and Secundilla, who, assigned to protect the Sallustian Gardens from Augustus Caesar's legions, were slain after a three-day siege and had their remains dragged through the streets.

The few that managed to reach the Brotherhood continued in the loyal service for years to come, never to be seen in the public eye again. At the Shrine, their new duties ranged from patrol of the secluded mountain passes to protecting the most sacred of relics—the Crystals of Uru.

The mystic Crystals date to an unknown time before the Lemurians. Contained within them are the truths and knowledge upon which the Brotherhood is based. No one person is in possession of all the knowledge they contain. A complete understanding of their content is rumored to cause physical death, for only when one is free of the constraints presented by a physical existence can one be free to explore the subtleties of truth. Thus, the knowledge of the Crystals was divided into a triad of equal leadership called the Aukhu.

One of the triad was Tog, a leader whose age was believed to equal that of the Crystals themselves. He was the holder of the spiritual realm. Itsu, a direct descendant of the Lemurians, was the keeper of the political affairs, guiding the world with his unseen agents. And lastly, there was Nof. The keeper of the sciences, he was careful in releasing the great secrets at a pace that could be safely assimilated by the general population. He knew of the great disasters which could unfold by "too much, too soon, too quickly."

It was the giant Sarius, with his gifted sense of perception and understanding, who first came to realize the evil intent of Itsu, the keeper of the world's affairs, and his followers. It was Sarius who noticed Itsu accessing the Crystals of Tog and Nof—a direct contradiction to the laws of Uru.

Sarius alerted others, but the alarm came too late. Itsu and his conspirators had already sunk their talons deeply into the heart of the organization. Those who resisted were slain. When it was over, the physical beings of Nof and Tog and Sarius had died, leaving Itsu as the leader of the Aukhu. He was to be known by a new name—the Hand Sinister.

Unhampered, he carefully absorbed as much from the Crystals as he could, without risking his own self-destruction. What little was left in the Crystals would remain unknown, for the Hand Sinister trusted no one.

The power shift complete, the Brotherhood moved onto a new and darker path, whose ultimate purpose was to gain an active, rather then a passive, control of the planet. He, the undying Itsu, would be the earth's new supreme leader.

The giants of the Nephilim, having been part of the resistance against Itsu, expected death to come quickly. Unfortunately for them, they were spared. The Hand Sinister had a new use for these colossal men.

Their tasks would be to invoke fear and terror among the general populace wherever needed. Knowing that they would resist such service, the Hand Sinister ordered the giants' minds to be forcibly altered through mind probes, hypnosis, and—in extreme cases—lobotomies.

Agent 13 knew that the Titan who towered over him was a descendant of these fabled men. The dullness in his eyes and the scar on his forehead told 13 that the man had been forcibly altered.

As the giant bent over him, 13 coolly assessed the huge man, looking for the fault, the point to strike at if and when the occasion arose.

"Search him," China's voice commanded.

The giant spun the shackled Agent over like a steak on a grill. 13 offered a token resistance.

"Hey! Nobody pads me!"

The giant found the object of his search—the Seer Stone. With a grunt of pleasure, he held it up proudly, his smile revealing a mutilated tongue.

Taking the pendant from the immense hand of her assistant, China examined the stone for a moment, then peered through it, studying her own palm.

"A fake," she said, tossing the stone to the floor.

"How dumb do you think I am?" Carson snarled groggily. "Think I'd bring it here so you and Stilts could wrestle it outta me? What kinda palooka yah take me for?"

"Show me his palms," China commanded.

Without a moment's delay, the giant spun 13 over on his belly and forced open the Agent's manacled, clenched fists.

Slowly China approached him, pulling her own Seer Stone from between her smooth, shapely breasts.

"Hey, what is this? You wanna see if my hands're clean or what?" Carson demanded, looking at China with a puzzled expression.

China ignored him. Lifting his hands, she gazed at the palms through the Stone. Her thoughts were visible on her face. First, a hungry kind of hope in her eyes. Then, disappointment, a faint regret. Finally, her eyes went back to ice blue.

13 snatched his hands away from hers. "Nobody does this to Michael Carson! Nobody!"

JAWS OF HORROR

China White turned away from the thug who was trying to blackmail her. Had she really expected to see the tattoo of the number that had at one time meant so much to her life?

Like the rest of the Brotherhood's top-level operatives, China White had heard the details of the murdered agents and theft of the Seer Stone in Istanbul. She had heard how the number 13 had been branded into the corpses' foreheads.

China shivered. Always before, the Brotherhood had been the hunters, never the hunted. But now *they* were the victims, and the man tracking them had been trained in their tactics and knew the organization well. Agent 13—the fallen angel, the Lucifer who fled from the Brotherhood so that he could strike back with a vengeance. He was dangerous, and he had to be stopped. But to China White, he was something more. . . .

The Seer Stone Carson had brought was a copy and a good one. It could only have been made from the Istanbul stone. So her conclusion that he might have been 13 in disguise was reasonable. But—did she really believe that the Agent would walk right into her den? No, of course not. But then, this Carson must be tied to 13 somehow.

13 knew that there were several Seer Stones in existence. All top Brotherhood agents carried

them. Certainly the Masque would have one. Therefore, he had prepared for the possibility of what had just occurred. Before leaving his lair in Washington D.C., 13 had applied a special new elastic imitation flesh over his hand. Identical to flesh in every way, it successfully hid his tell-tale tattoo of the Brotherhood. Then he had attached the fake Seer Stone Ray produced to the golden chain of the original. Finally, he'd hidden the real Seer Stone in a place that was known only to him, certain that the Brotherhood dared not kill him until they had regained possession of the stone.

"Help him up," China commanded the giant. "Show Mr. Carson to a proper seat."

No sooner had she uttered the commands than 13 felt the massive hands of the giant tightening around his waist. Suddenly his body was lifted from the cold floor and dumped into one of the black lacquer chairs in front of China's desk.

"That's better. Now, how 'bout these bracelets?"

"Soon, Mr. Carson. First, I'd like to ask you some questions."

"Listen, toots, I got somethin' you and Stilts here want pretty bad. Now, I'm not happy, you're not happy. I want money, you want the rock. It sounds like a pretty simple deal to me, and judging by the look of the place, you can certainly afford the price. So, if you're done with the rustle, then we can get down to business."

China was silent, staring into the water. 13 had leisure to study her.

Time had only made her more beautiful. None of the brutal intrigue that surrounded her had left its mark. The sound of a buzzer suddenly disturbed the tranquillity.

China reached behind her desk and brought a telephone receiver to her ear. "Yes?"

13 watched her face, trying to deduce what was being said by the voice on the other end. But China's face remained smooth and cold.

"I see," she said into the mouthpiece after listening several moments. "Proceed with your plan." With that, she hung up the receiver.

Picking up the fake Seer Stone, she said, "Again, how did you get this?"

"I made it from the original."

"And where's the original?"

Carson grinned. "I gotta spell it out?"

China looked at him, bored.

"We agree on a price," Carson said as though talking to a stupid child. "You hand me the money. I tell you where the rock is."

"Tell me how you came by the original."

Carson sighed. "Jeez! All right, if it's so damn important. We was waitin' to strike. I was lookin' inside the room and seen this film fellow standing up, holding the rock out and startin' to talk 'bout secret societies and stuff. I was thinkin' 'what a wacko.' Then he goes into this long hurrah about invisible tattoos and whatnot. I tell ya, the guy was full of more hot air than a weather balloon. Anyway, we let 'em gab till the clock started dingin', then we turned the room into stringed beef, just like we was told. When it was all over, I grabbed the rock. It looked like it might'a been worth something. And that's the story."

"Was he killed in the attack?" China asked, her voice losing some of its coolness.

"Who? The palooka with the flapping jaw?"

China nodded.

"The only people who left that room were measured for boxes."

"Are you sure?"

"When the guy's lying in blood, you look in his eye and see nothin' but milkshake spillin' out, you don't go checking for bullet-proof jackets."

"Maybe you should next time."

"Why's that?"

"Because Kent Walters is alive and recovering at Bethesda Naval Hospital."

Carson began to fidget in his seat. "That—that's crazy!" he blustered. "I tell ya nothin' coulda' survived that curtain of lead!"

"My sources are never wrong, Mr. Carson—if that is who you are. . . ."

"Whaddya talkin' 'bout? Sure it's who I am!"

China returned to her desk and pressed a button beneath it. The large mirror behind her desk slowly became a transparent window, opening on a chamber hidden on the other side.

A large, black iron chair stood in the center of the room. A pale-skinned woman was sitting in the device, held by tight leather straps binding her at her wrists, waist, and ankles. An iron helmet fully enshrouded her head and secured it firmly to the chair back. Electrical wires ran from the helmet's back into what appeared to be a high voltage generator.

Two fiends wearing lab jackets—one a dwarf, the other a chunky, leering, older man—stood nearby, making final adjustments to the straps and their machinery. 13 had seen the device before—it was called the Helmet of Truth.

Through a process of electrical shock and thought inducement, the helmetlike device could manifest the subject's worst imaginable fears and nightmares. These horrific images, or hallucinations, would appear to the victim to be real events whose temporal setting was the present.

The intensity and horror could be controlled through manipulation of the in-going current. Too much of the "treatment" could lead to permanent brain damage or death. But when used by a skilled hand, it could break the toughest of hoods.

As Leer nodded, the dwarf threw a switch. The woman suddenly froze with electrified horror. Her fingers gripped the iron armrests, knuckles white with fear. The sounds of her screams couldn't be heard through the helmet and the glass, but he knew they were there.

The dwarf shut down the machine, and Leer lifted the helmet from the woman's head. She slumped forward, but not before 13 had seen her face. A shudder ran through him. Although her body and dress were those of a young, lovely woman, she now had the face of a hag of ninety. Her hair had turned white; her skin was horribly wrinkled, aged with fear; her eyes were frozen in unmoving, lingering terror.

13 didn't have to act to make Carson's features register horror.

China turned away from her desk and walked back toward the handcuffed Agent as the window clouded back into a mirror.

"The device is called the Helmet of Truth. Like you, that woman was hired by us to perform a task. She didn't do the job. Instead, she fled with the money we had fronted her. She didn't get far. Like you, she told us lies and attempted to extort money from us!"

"You people are sick!"

"All we want is the truth and—as you can see— we have ways of getting it."

13 tensed as he noticed the water's green reflection slowly turning red along the surface of China's black marble desk. Turning, he looked out the window. Gallons of blood and dismembered cow parts were slowly drifting down from the surface. The water's reflection took on a ghastly hue, filling the room with a crimson-red light.

A great white shark suddenly swam into view.

"Have you ever seen sharks in a feeding frenzy?" China's voice sounded as if she were giving a disinterested lecture.

"No! And I've had enough of you and your fancy threats. Now you either make the deal or you don't, but if I don't go walkin' outta here in five minutes, my boys are comin' in to get me!"

"Your boys?" China remarked coolly.

"That's right, sugar! Fifty of 'em, coming here to tear this place apart."

The great white struck at a slab of descending beef and bone, whipping it from side to side in its viselike jaws. Several other great whites shot out of the water's darkness, looking for similar treats.

"Lovely creatures," China remarked as she watched. "Nature's most perfect feeding machines. Their evolution has changed little in ten million years."

Carson made a feeble attempt to rise from his seat, but the giant grabbed the Agent's shoulders with his massive hands, forcing him down.

"Stay, Mr Carson. I'm sure this will be a show that you'll enjoy." China turned to her assistant. "Please give our guest a better view."

The giant picked up the Agent and the chair, easily carrying them both to the nearby window.

Outside the glass plates, more sharks arrived, darting through the bloody water and lights in a frenzied dance of death. The windows buckled and shook as the creatures slammed against them in turmoil. Then there was a huge surge of water against the glass. A huge black object drifted downward.

"Why, here comes one of your boys to the rescue now!" China mocked.

Agent 13 watched in horror as the object entered the realm of artificial light. It was his rented DeSoto! The vehicle came to a gentle stop on the sandy bottom near the windows. Trapped inside the auto, gasping and struggling for the final breaths from a diminishing air pocket, was the terrified Ray Furnow.

The Agent knew Ray had two choices—he could either suffocate when the air ran out, or he could take his chance with the great white sharks by leaving the car and breaking for the surface.

China was watching him closely.

"I don't think the others will be coming, do you?" she asked.

13 didn't reply. His mind raced through his options. Getting out of the handcuffs presented little problem. What occupied him more was figuring out a way to get to Ray before it was too late.

China turned from the window and slowly approached him. "Now, why don't you tell me who you are and who you really work for?"

The giant's grip tightened on his shoulders. 13 swallowed hard. The masquerade was over. Even if China believed he wasn't Agent 13, she also knew he wasn't Carson. And if they knew about Ray, they also knew about Maggie. . . .

13 was alone and without a gun. His poison ring and heel dagger would be of little use against the hybrid giant, whose immense size would dilute and slow the potency of the poisons. But it didn't matter. There were other, more effective, "tools" available to him.

His mind raced backward in time to his days at the Shrine, to the training sessions when he'd had to defend himself against ten armed attackers at once. There was no room for error—to have failed would have meant death. The Brotherhood wasn't interested in agents of lesser abilities. But 13 had survived and excelled. He was their best.

Agent 13 relaxed. His joints and muscles became pliable. His hands slid free of the handcuffs like a knife sliding out of warm butter. He grasped the freed manacles in his hands. His years of training had taught him how to turn any object into a lethal weapon.

The giant's enormous height forced him to bend over as he held the Agent firmly in the chair. Knowing that the giant's weight was slightly displaced, the Agent threw his own shoulders into dislocation, causing the giant to fall forward, slightly off balance. It was all that was needed. During the split second the giant struggled to regain his leverage, 13 broke free. Snapping his shoulders back into place, the Agent spun to face his towering opponent.

He quickly thrust upward with the serrated edge of the handcuffs. The makeshift weapon tore through the giant's clothing and entered his abdomen just below his sternum. The giant, caught off guard, let out a low, painful gasp as 13 continued to jam the lethal instrument up toward his heart. The giant swung at his tormentor. The blow drone the Agent across the cold iron floor.

The giant howled in pain as he grabbed at the handcuffs dangling from his chest cavity. Spinning and twisting around the room out of control, he looked like a trout trying to free itself from a fisherman's hook.

13 pulled himself back to his feet. Out of the corner of his eye, he could see China reaching behind her desk and pulling out a pistol. Its distinctive shape told him it was a long-barreled Mauser. She leveled and fired as the Agent leaped for the nearest shield he could find—the giant.

The shot missed, but only because of the Agent's catlike reflexes. The slug slammed into the plate glass holding back the sea. A small bullet impact hole appeared in the surface of the window. The tremendous weight of the water caused the sea water to jet into the room in a stinging, pencil-thin stream.

China fired twice more. One flashed over the Agent's shoulder, the other hit the giant in the thigh. The man twisted in confusion as he swung again at the Agent and missed.

Apparently, the giant was expendable, for China fired again—this time right at the giant, hitting him in the hand. He fled backward, clutching his hand and howling in pain while trying to avoid the gunshots. The Agent stayed close to him. Dimly figuring that 13 was responsible for his problems, the giant swung at him again with his deadly, hammerlike fists. The Agent dived out of the way, landing beneath the stream of water being forced through the bullet hole.

China held her fire for fear of hitting the window again. The giant saw his chance. Rage built within him as he lunged at the fallen Agent. Suddenly his feet slipped on the wet floor and the giant's enormous bulk slammed head first into the window. The plate buckled under the force. A screeching sound suddenly filled the chamber.

Everyone in the room stared at the window, which had a new six-foot crack from the bullet hole to the lower corner. Small tricklets of water first seeped, then jetted through the crack.

The faltering giant pushed himself up slowly from the floor, putting his mangled, blood-drenched hand against the window for support.

A fifteen-foot shark, seeing the motion, lunged at the window with its thrashing jaws. The shark's impact sent another crack screeching through the glass pane. Small, growing streams of sea water began to shoot out along the length of the two cracks, but the strong metal bands held the glass in place. Frustrated, the massive shark circled back into the darkness. Finer cracks suddenly appeared as the window started to give way.

There was sudden movement in the room. Agent 13 looked over at China White, only to catch a fleeting glimpse of her as she escaped through a revolving wall panel behind her desk. The giant, it appeared, had an instinct for survival. Forgetting about the Agent, he ran to the doors, hoping for an exit, but they were sealed and locked. Even his great strength couldn't force them open.

The chamber echoed with the moaning of the buckling window as needle shards of splintering glass shot from the cracks. 13 ran to the panel through which China had disappeared. It was secure and refused to budge. Turning, he slammed his body's full weight against the mirror. It was solid as a wall. 13 looked back at the cracked window. The giant was there, futilely holding his massive hands against the glass, hoping to keep the cracking plates in place. Blood and jetting water were everywhere.

Then something swam into view. The giant looked beyond his crimson hands, beyond the plated glass, and into the massive sea that he was attempting to hold back. He glimpsed his fate. A huge great white shark moved from the inky blackness like a torpedo. The monster's grisly jaws opened wide as its speed increased. Its cold, dead eyes locked onto the giant's bleeding form as it sped toward the window.

The giant backed away in horror, trying to retreat to the back of the room. Seeing what was bound to happen, 13 leaped onto China's desk, jumping from there up to the ceiling, where he grabbed hold of an iron beam just as the shark, driven wild by rage, crashed into the window.

The metal bands buckled, and the pane shattered. The tremendous pressure of the water shot into the room, carrying the shark directly at the giant like a rocket riding the airstream. Striking the giant in the back, the shark's massive serrated teeth dug deeply into his flesh as the pressure slammed them against the opposite wall.

The door the Agent had entered burst away, blown off its hinges by the powerful pressure. The waters rushed up the stairwell in an inverted whirlpool of destruction.

The shark, sucked by the water from its hold on the giant, was sent spinning and thrashing. The giant held on to a wall beam for support as the water gushed inward. But even his great strength gave way. He was sucked down, toward the staircase, fighting and struggling.

Suddenly the rushing waters grew calm; having filled the room to the window and door-frame level, an equalized pressure had been obtained. An eerie silence settled over the room, broken only by the rhythmic, dying surges of the water.

13 lay along the iron ceiling beam, breathing from a large pocket of trapped air. The ceiling light beside him flickered its last moments as 13 watched the giant who refused to die pull himself from the depths to share the pocket of air. The giant's respite was short-lived, however.

With the water calm, the great white moved in to claim his prize.

The waters churned and boiled a frothy red as the two giants spun and twisted in a match for survival. But the human giant had been injured too many times, and the world he was fighting in belonged to the shark.

Try as he might, the massive man couldn't break the beast's iron grip. With a final gasp, he was dragged down for the last time.

13 realized he had to get of there, fast! The shark would take a few minutes to devour the

giant, then it would look for its next snack. And there was still Ray, somewhere out there. It was only a matter of moments until Ray's air supply was exhausted, if it wasn't already. And Maggie— what sinister fate had she met in his absence?

He carefully slid along the upper beam. Positioning himself so that he was directly above the shattered window, he began concentrating on lowering his breathing rate, thereby reducing his need for air. Using such techniques would permit him to remain under water for up to three minutes. He glanced about for the sharks. They still appeared to be feasting in the far corner. With great resolve, 13 took his last breath and gently slid into the chilling waters.

The water tasted of blood and death. He swam in slow, evenly measured strokes, trying not to attract the attention of the feeding beasts.

The blurry image of the sunken DeSoto loomed in the distance. 13 fought against the strong tidal currents that snaked between the large pylons and threatened to carry him out to sea.

Seconds counted and his progress slowed to a near stop. He fought down the urge to break for the surface. Only after an incredible effort was he able to reach the car. He was too late.

Ray was gone. Only a pilot fish, who seemed to have laid claim to the new home, was to be found in the car. The Agent didn't have time to carry on a search for his trusted assistant—or what was left of him. His lungs screamed for air, his head began to burn. Soon, the sharks would be returning to the business of eating.

Lungs bursting, Agent 13 swam upward toward the surface. . . .

DANCE IN THE DELUGE

While Agent 13 went to his fateful meeting with China White, Maggie Darr studied the slobbering thug beside her at the mahogany bar like a panther eyeing game from a tree branch.

Somehow, the one-eyed slickster seemed familiar to her.

"What's your monicker?" she asked.

"Jack Spade, on account that I only got one eye, like the Jack of Spades," he said, jamming his cigar into his lips and sticking his hand out.

Maggie shook hands with him. The name meant nothing to her. He moved closer, the smell of gin on his breath.

"Say, yer a real good looker." Spade leered. "Yer wasted on Carson, dollface." A sudden thought seemed to cross his mind. He said, grinning, "I'll bet you look great in a swim suit. What would you say to an ocean voyage?"

Leaning close, he tried to put his hand around Maggie's waist. She coyly slipped out.

"What was that about an ocean voyage?" she said, backing up slightly.

"It's a job on the *Normandie*," he said.

Maggie raised her eyebrows. "A 'job'?" she said, sneering. "You gotta *work* for a ride?"

"You don't call it work, not on the biggest, classiest ship sailin' the ocean. I'm runnin' cards outta a suite. It's easy pickin's, the tub's packed

with Mainliners and other high-muckity-mucks.
Hell, the Babe's gonna be on the ship, along with a
few Astors and Vanderbilts. Heck, China's even
gonna make the scene."

"China White?"

"Only one I know of."

"Is that so?" Maggie asked with interest.

"I tell ya, any flimflammer can make a killin'."
He winked. "Maybe even you. . . ."

"Yah think so?" Maggie smacked her gum.

"The ship don't sail till Tuesday." Jack Spade
reached into his pocket and produced a ticket
folder for passage on the *Normandie*. "I got two
tickets, First Class."

Moving closer, he slipped the tickets into her
hand for inspection.

"I'm lookin' for a good dish to help me pull 'em
in, if ya know what I mean."

He placed his hand on the inside of her thigh
and patted it twice.

Maggie hauled off and slapped Spade across the
face. "Whaddya take me for? I ain't no floozie, I'll
tell you that!"

"Easy, babe," Jack said soothingly. "You don't
have to do nothin' but meet the softs in the bar,
feel 'em out, drop a coupla hooks, then reel 'em
into the room for the game."

"What's in it for me?" Maggie asked, holding up
a cigarette at the long end of a diamond-studded
holder for Spade to light.

"Ten percent of the take," he said.

"I don't know . . . There's Mickie. . . ."

"What's there to know? It's like shootin' fish in
a barrel. I'm tellin' you, it's the easiest money
you'll ever see. As for Mickie, he's a loser. China'll
take care a him."

"Oh, yeah?" Maggie asked casually. "What
does that mean?"

"Never you mind, sweets. Just don't worry about the clod, that's all."

Maggie froze, wondering what Spade meant. Somehow, she had to find out what was going on!

Maggie's attention was drawn to a pair of doors at the far end of the crowded, smoke-filled room. Three large thugs from the establishment were working their way through the crowd, checking out the women one by one. Somehow, Maggie had a feeling they weren't looking for dates for the evening. They seemed particularly interested in blondes. . . . Turning around, she fired a dirty look at the fat drinker who sat next to her.

"Ya gettin' an earful, Mack?" she said coldly. Flouncing off her bar seat angrily, she looked at Spade. "Ya think we could go somewhere more private?"

Spade's eyes lit up. "No problem!" He signaled to the bartender.

The attentive bartender—an older, balding man with a whiskey-reddened nose—was quick to respond. "Another round, Mister Spade?"

"Got any rooms, Barney?"

"Three left."

"Gimme your best, and tab it."

"Whatever you say, Mister Spade." The bartender signaled to a nearby waiter. "Show Mister Spade and his friend to the Sheik's Tent."

The waiter quickly led them through the crowd to a hallway in the back of the establishment. Maggie looked back at the thugs, who continued to search the crowd. She hadn't been seen.

Jack caught one of her nervous glances.

"Still worried about your friend?" He sneered.

"What 'friend'?" she said, taking Jack's arm.

He laughed raucously.

Several closed doors led off the hallway. The waiter opened one of them and parted a heavy curtain, then stood back.

"You're gonna love this place!" Jack informed her as he entered the room.

Maggie paused. It was like walking into the Arabian Nights. The walls were covered in Persian tapestries, the floors in rich, hand-woven rugs. Large, overstuffed pillows covered low couches that encircled the room. In the center was a large, circular, brass-hammered table, on which sat a tall water pipe with multiple hoses. The room was perfumed with exotic incense . . . and something else—the smell of hashish.

Maggie entered the room to find a man, attired in Turkish Scimiteer clothing, standing at attention in the corner.

"I thought this was private," she said to Jack, pouting.

"Part of the show. Here to serve." Jack smiled and pulled Maggie down on the couch beside him. "Besides, the guy's a mute. He ain't goin' be repeatin' nothin' we say to nobody."

"He makes me nervous." Maggie sniffed. "Tell 'im to cart out."

"Relax."

Jack snapped his fingers. The Scimiteer produced a bottle of champagne and held it out. With his other hand, he flashed his sword. The cork popped like a gunshot and bounced off the ceiling as a tall plume of champagne flew across the room, dousing the table.

The Scimiteer quickly sheathed his blade and bent down to pick up a pair of champagne glasses. In an instant, he caught the flowing wine in the glass and presented it to Maggie Darr.

Giggling in pretended delight, Maggie took the glass. As she did so, however, she looked directly into the Scimiteer's eyes. Startled, she saw there a disturbing mixture—numbness, distance, evil.

Was he a Jinda? Or just a hood? Or maybe nothing, just her imagination? He turned away, going back to his post by the wall.

Turning back to Jack, Maggie raised her glass and smiled.

Jack smiled, too—a devilish, wolfish smile.

Maggie couldn't be sure whether the Scimiteer had seen her pour the first two glasses of champagne into the fern by the big velvet pillow she was leaning against while the gangster wrapped his arm around her. But he couldn't have missed the third time, for she leaned over at an awkward angle, hoping Spade felt as if she were caressing him, while she was, in reality, dumping the drink.

Spade slipped his hand up the long slit of Maggie's skirt.

Her knee came up and caught him in the chin, causing him to bite his tongue.

"Oops, sorry, accident," she said sweetly.

Spade glared at her, wiping blood from his chin. "Listen, blondie, there's a lot more where you came from. If you're not gonna play the game, you're gonna get hurt!" He pulled at her hair to remind her who was who, but it flew off in his hand. Spade stared at the wig for a moment in shock, then began to roar with laughter.

"Your hair's as phony as you are! But I'll betcha there's parts of you that are real!" With that, he grabbed the front of her gown.

Not wanting to break cover, Maggie shouted, glancing over at the Scimiteer. "Help me!"

As if made of wood, he stood, staring silently ahead, apparently having seen it all before.

Bracing her foot against Spade's chest, she shoved him backward. His clutching fingers tore her gown to her waist as he slammed back against the pillows, propelled by her foot.

A grim laugh came from his blood-stained teeth. "I love watching 'em squirm!" he said to nobody in particular.

Then, his single eye flashed as Maggie jumped to her feet. "Wait," he said, gasping. "That red hair! I seen you before!"

In a cold moment of recognition, Maggie realized why he had looked familiar. On the night of Fats Milligan's bachelor party, when she had popped up from the cake with the grease gun, he had been one of the faces in the crowd.

As she raked the room, she caught him in the eye. He crawled away. She was about to dust him, but he begged for his life, holding one hand over his bleeding eye. Since he wasn't part of Lucky's gang, Maggie had been merciful.

Now, she regretted it. Lucky's gang had come back to haunt her.

Maggie dove for her purse as the gangster dove for her. He grabbed her ankle.

"You marked me!" Spade said, spitting blood from his mouth. "I done nothing and you whanged me in the eye!"

"You were in the wrong crowd," she said with a husky voice, kicking her foot in a try to break free.

"That still don't call for this!" he said. Still hanging on to her firmly with one hand, with the other he pulled away his eye patch to reveal a ghastly purple socket where an eye should have been. Then, he drew a buck knife.

"I'll show you what it is to be mutilated!" he roared, dragging Maggie toward him.

The hell with her cover. It was blown anyhow. Her hand had hold of her purse. Ceasing her struggles, Maggie pretended to be weak with fear, letting Spade pull her toward him.

"I know it doesn't count for much," Maggie began babbling, to keep him occupied as her hand fished around inside her purse. "But I had a score to settle with Milligan."

"Oh, yeah?" He ran the flat of the knife blade up over her arm.

"Yeah. We-we had a badger game going."

He laughed.

Maggie continued, talking feverishly. "I'd lead 'em into the room, start showin' 'em a good time, and he catches the whole thing on film."

"Pretty cheap scam, even for Fats."

"Cheap, yeah, but safe. Most of 'em were married and didn't want to have hotel room stuff come up."

Damn! Her gun wasn't there! It must have spilled out onto the floor during their struggle. Her fingers felt around. Her gun was out of reach. But an atomizer of perfume wasn't.

Jack Spade glared down at her. "That don't explain rakin' a room, sister!"

Swinging her hand up, Maggie sprayed her perfume into Spade's one good eye.

Spade let out a loud shriek and grabbed for his burning eye. Using the training Agent 13 had taught her, Maggie jammed his elbows upward with one hand while she struck him in the Adam's apple with the other. Then she wriggled off the couch and dove for her pistol.

Spade gagged and recoiled, giving Maggie time to jump to her feet, her gun leveled, her eyes on both Spade and the still-unmoving Scimiteer.

"Take it easy and no one gets hurt," she said.

She was backing for the door when, suddenly, it opened, and what appeared to be a pin-stripe wall stepped in.

"Going somewhere, sweetie?" the harsh voice said as huge arms grabbed her from behind.

Pin-stripe started to squeeze. Maggie still held the gun, but she couldn't move it. Her upper arms and chest were being slowly caved in.

Jack Spade struggled to his feet.

"You've done your last damage, dame!"

Ripping the gun out of her hand, Spade slapped her across the mouth. Then he turned to the impassive Scimiteer.

"Go get Rudy. He's got a corpse to deal with."

The mute Scimiteer left the room.

The odds were suddenly better. Spade let out a loud groan as Maggie's foot kicked him square in the solar plexus, knocking his breath out. The gun flew up in the air as he stumbled.

In the same flash of movement, Maggie's foot came down hard, her pump heel burying deep into Pin-stripe's instep.

"Bitch!" he screamed, as he momentarily eased his grip. Maggie spun and twisted free, grabbing her gun up as it hit the floor.

Pin-stripe's hand disappeared into his jacket and a gun appeared in a flash of silver. But he was too slow. Maggie's finger closed over her trigger. A shot rang out, and Pin-stripe stood stupidly as a third eye opened in his forehead.

Jack Spade crawled toward her, shouting for help. Ignoring him, Maggie ran through a door and found herself on the dance floor of the club. Spade's voice rang out. Two thugs lunged for her when, suddenly, Maggie heard a loud crack.

A door burst open, and water cascaded into the room. The dance floor was caught in the flash flood. Scrambling up onto a piano, Maggie jumped for a chandelier as the waters swirled beneath her.

The room went dark. Screams were drowned out in the rushing torrents of water. The tidal wave overflowed the stage and splashed against the far wall. Clinging to the chandelier, Maggie saw people clamoring up on top of the mirrored stage while water swirled around them.

There was nowhere for her to go, apparently. Desperate, her arms throbbing with the strain, Maggie reached up to the ceiling above her and felt around. Suddenly she gasped in relief. There, within reach of the chandelier, was a ceiling vent!

Climbing the chain of the chandelier, Maggie reached the ceiling vent. Using her earring as a screwdriver, she unscrewed the cover and, with a strength born of desperation, pulled herself wearily up into the ventilation pipe.

She leaned back against the shaft, her legs straightened to hold her in place as she tried to catch her breath and ease the pain in her arms.

Where was 13? She didn't dare think about it. She had to keep going. She didn't have much time—it wouldn't be long before the whole building collapsed.

Propelling herself up the ventilation shaft, Maggie reached the main floor of the Brown Rat. Most of the patrons had guessed something was wrong, though no one knew yet what it was. The bartenders were working frantically to clear the building. No one noticed as Maggie kicked out the grillwork. A moment later, she was free.

Outside the Brown Rat, a river of fleeing people emptied into a sea of onlookers. Maggie glanced at the parking lot. Their car was gone! A quick search of the crowd revealed no sign of either 13 or Ray.

Then, Maggie saw some of China White's thugs studying the crowd. Could they still be searching for her? She didn't dare hang around.

Sliding away, she disappeared into the shadows.

DEATH WAITS ALONE

A flurry of stars flickered over the Imperial Palace Hotel. By night, lit only by the ambient light of stars and moon, it seemed a regal structure. But when the hard light of day fell upon it, revealing its peeling paint, cracking cement, and broken windows, the hotel gave away her age.

When the Imperial Palace in New York was built, Grover Cleveland inhabited the White House. It had been a fine establishment, catering to the rich and famous of Europe and America alike. But her glory was not to last. Years of disinterested management ran it into the ground, and the Depression reduced the once grand dame to destitution.

By 1937, the hotel crawled with those dregs of society who could afford a dollar a night and did not mind erratic heating, testy plumbing, the skittering rodent, or the occasional ghost here and there.

For everyone knew the hotel was haunted.

In 1886, when the hotel was in her glory, a terrible incident had occurred in it. Harold Stanton, a California railroad magnate, ran into financial troubles and came east to persuade bankers to prop him up. Armed with dozens of letters of introduction, Stanton traipsed up and down Wall Street, trying to interest bankers in his plan to create the largest railroad monopoly in North

America.

At first, his plan stirred great interest, but rumors about his financial woes reached the East Coast. The warm greetings became chilly rebuffs. Dinner invitations became unreturned messages. Still Stanton persisted, but eventually the magnate's funds ran out.

In the depths of winter, he fell behind on his hotel bill. Claiming that he was awaiting an overdue check from California, Stanton was allowed an extension. When the second due date came, the manager sadly, respectfully, and dutifully informed Stanton that he would have to vacate his rooms on the following morning.

As the sun rose, bellboys, maids, manager, and clerk eagerly awaited Stanton's appearance, filled with morbid curiosity to know what a man who had dropped from the height above them to destitution below them would have to say for himself.

By 11:00 a.m., Stanton had not graced the lobby, and the manager—a meek, timid man—ordered a chambermaid to enter his apartment and remind him of his departure time.

Fearful of losing her job, she had no choice but to obey. When a knock on the door received no answer, she entered the room with a passkey. She came upon a sight that would torment her for years to come. Stanton hung from the chandelier in his suite.

Irony fell upon irony. The friends who had never sent Stanton the money he needed in life lavished it upon his funeral, hoping to ease their guilt.

Once news of his suicide was made public, telegrams poured in. The magnate's funeral was the highlight of New York's social season. Meanwhile, New York society quickly turned upon the "heartless" hotel. The manager went into isolation and eventually died in his own hotel under mysterious circumstances. The Imperial was rumored to be hexed.

In a weak effort to make amends, Myron Hartford, the owner of the hotel, arranged to have the room where Stanton died sealed off, vowing that it would remain unoccupied forever.

Though the taint of the incident hung over the hotel for a long time (and may well have been a contributing factor to its subsequent fall from grace), the incident that caused it had been forgotten. Still boarded up, the cursed room itself was avoided by even the most hardened vagrant.

13, however, found the reports about the incident during one of his many searches through the newspaper morgue. He had used this method to discover other hideouts and secret rooms, searching through old records for abandoned buildings, sealed-off rooms, houses tied up in lost wills and estates.

After an investigation of the old hotel, he knew that the location would be perfect for a lair. He was able to devise a swinging brick wall that would permit him entrance into the sealed room from the neighboring flophouse.

The room became one of three bases for Agent 13's New York operations. The hotel's location afforded 13 access to the seedier sections of the city.

Maggie Darr stared through the small window of the dark room, watching the sleeping city. Though she was both warm and dry, she was still wrapped in blankets, and her hands trembled.

She had been waiting for Agent 13 for hours now. It was their agreed meeting spot in case their plans went awry.

The room was just the same as when it had been sealed years before. It looked expensive, old, and dusty. 13 had no use for the comfort of the plush red-velvet couches and chairs. The only sign of his presence was a large corner filled with his weapons, files, and disguises.

As the minutes ticked slowly, agonizingly by, Maggie tore her gaze from the darkness outside, looking at his things as if she could will him back. What would she do if he failed to return? Her heart felt the distant murmur of pain.

Hours passed. Day dawned. She listened for his footstep, but it didn't come and there was no word from him. She knew that, if he were alive, he would have contacted her somehow. No, he was dead. She would have to accept that. Ray must be dead, too.

Maggie slumped on the couch, wrapped in the blanket. What should she do? Where could she go? A sudden draft wafted into the room as floor boards creaked.

Maggie leaped to her feet.

"You!" she cried, startled.

It was 13—cold, alone, and alive.

"Good, you're here," he said without emotion.

Maggie, nonplussed at this casual response, came to a halt just as she had been about to fling her arms around him. Something in his face told her this would be highly unwelcome. Gulping, Maggie managed to shrug.

"Sure," she said in her best Crystal-the-floozie voice. "I'm here. Whaddya expect?"

If he caught her sarcasm, 13 let it pass without comment. Unable to keep from breathing a trembling sigh of relief, Maggie hurried to help the Agent remove his wet clothes. He normally would have rebuked her teasingly for such fussing over him, but this time he didn't say a word. His face was a blank, even beneath its mask.

Maggie went colder than 13. Something had

happened to him, something that had affected him deeply. Was it his encounter with China White? She couldn't bring herself to ask. She couldn't make herself say that name. Maybe that wasn't it at all. Maybe it was something else.

"Ray?" she asked gently.

"Either dead or fleeing from his wives, I don't know—" 13 said coldly.

Maggie swallowed, chilled by the coolness of his response. Would he have reacted the same way if it were Ray asking about *her* disappearance? she wondered bleakly.

Moodily, 13 threw on a dressing gown she handed to him. He seemed preoccupied, worried.

"I learned that China White is sailing on the *Normandie*," Maggie said brightly, hoping for a reaction that might lift him from the gloom.

It worked.

"Where did you hear that?"

"Some greaseball at the Rat said that she was going to be on the ship," Maggie said, pleased to see him liven up.

"That's it!" 13 cried. And, just as the water had gushed through the broken window pane, Agent 13 began to pour forth a torrent of words, talking so fast that Maggie had trouble following his tale.

13 told her of his meeting with China White, even alluding to the moments they had shared years ago, though he did not go into these in detail.

He told her of his fruitless five-hour search of the bay for some sign of Ray's body. It was only after dawn that he had called off his search and returned to the lair. But first, he did one last thing. He had stopped in a phone booth to call Benny the Eye, who was still busy tailing Dr. Fischer.

"Some foreign-looking types with German accents met with Fischer last night at his place,"

Benny reported. "The bug I planted worked perfectly. The Nazis are all hot for this Lightning Gun of his, and they want to see a demonstration. They're talkin' big bucks. More'n this prof'll see in a lifetime of teachin' losers. They gave him a ticket—First Class—"

"For the *Normandie!*" Maggie cried triumphantly.

13 nodded. Suddenly it was beginning to make sense, the pieces were falling together. The Brotherhood wanted Fischer, that much was plain. The next disaster? What more horrible incident than to destroy the wealthiest, most lavish luxury liner the world had ever known—especially since it would be loaded with celebrities. 13 saw the simplicity of the plan. Hundreds, thousands might die. And, in the confusion, who would miss Dr. Fischer? He would be presumed dead.

13 swore in frustration. He saw the elements of the plan, but how to stop it?

There was always the alternative of killing Fischer, but he didn't have time. The *Normandie* sailed tomorrow. He would have to take his grim business aboard the ship. But would killing Fischer stop the disaster? Not likely. And how would he get onto the *Normandie* anyhow? At this late date, it would be impossible to get tickets. 13 considered his options carefully. He'd have to call in more than a few favors. . . .

"What are you grinning that idiotic smile for?" he snapped at Maggie irritably. "Don't you realize how serious—"

13 stopped.

"Two tickets . . . on the *Normandie*," Maggie Darr said smoothly, holding them up. "First Class."

19

VESSEL OF LIGHT

Between the years 1912 and 1929, the French ruled the seas of luxury passenger liner service with three ships—the *France,* launched in 1912; the *Paris,* launched in 1921; and the *Ile de France,* launched in 1927. With these ships, the French dominated the lucrative and ever-growing market of transatlantic service.

The year 1928 had been a banner year for the line. During that year, they transported over ninety thousand passengers, and receipts exceeded a billion francs, with over half coming from its New York service alone. Other countries, seeing the potential for profit, took notice and entered the growing marketplace.

Germany tossed her hat into the ring in 1929 with the launchings of the *Bremen* and the *Europa.* Modern, quicker, and larger, the ships sliced into the French Line's profits, England commissioned work on a new liner to be called the *Queen Mary.* The French were losing their market.

France needed a new ship. Work began on the vessel that would become the largest, fastest, and most luxurious vessel ever to sail the seas. Her name—SS *Normandie.*

One thousand twenty-nine feet in length, the *Normandie* was capable of attaining a speed well over thirty-two knots. She weighed as much as several Eiffel Towers and, if stood on her bow, measured taller than the Empire State Building. She could carry two thousand passengers—eight hundred and fifty of them in First Class.

But she was not only functional, she was beautiful as well. Artwork by Dupas, Dunand, Jouve, and Gernez adorned her corridors. The tables were set with crystal by Rene Lalique, silver by Puiforcat. The elegant furniture and tapestries were by Gaudissart. Journalists called the *Normandie* "The Eighth Wonder of the World," "The Vessel of Light," "The Floating Versailles," and the "Messenger of Peace."

"Messenger of Peace . . ." It could be a "Messenger of Death. . . ."

It was a busy afternoon at the French Line pier in New York Harbor. Cars, limos, and cabs queued up, waiting to unload their passengers. Baggage handlers pushed heavily laden carts past the bow of the great ship.

Standing atop the gangway was Night Watch Officer Renard, a dashing Frenchman in his mid-thirties, who had the distinction of being known as a "Ladies' Man." Conscious of his swarthy good looks and the fine fit of his Paris-tailored uniform, Renard smiled effusively at the boarding passengers—informing them of the meticulous service they could expect to receive.

Standing near the First Class gangway, Renard reveled in the reflected glory of the illustrious people walking past him. It was the cream of 1937 society—Mr. and Mrs. Douglas Fairbanks (taking a European vacation while attending the opening of his new film in Paris); Mr. William C. Bullitt, the U.S. Ambassador (returning to France after his latest briefing on the "German situation"); the famous Vogue model, Mlle. Delamarre, and her fawning "escort," Michael Richardson, a wealthy

American industrialist. Behind them came such diverse notables as Cary Grant; the Maharajah Manikya of Tripura; the painter, Salvador Dali; the author, Antoine de Saint-Exupéry. The *Normandie* had become "the only way to cross."

Officer Renard considered himself a master of human nature. For many, this was an amusing hobby. For Renard, it was a career. Being the officer of the night watch, he was able to gain a great deal by knowing who was willing to pay what for what or who was lonely for his company in the wee, small hours.

Renard had spent many pleasant nights comforting newly divorced movie actresses, young starlets seeking time away from aged producer husbands, new brides who married for money and begged for affection. Renard had pocketed many, many dollars from men who traded love for money as well as those who traded in poker chips. Renard enjoyed his job, especially the fringe benefits.

So, Renard kept an eagle eye on all boarding passengers, classifying them, slotting them in his mind, making a running commentary on each.

"Young wife, jewels, old husband. Mmmm. She will be needing company, I have no doubt. And that so very chic gentleman is a gambler, and not an honest one. Perhaps, one of Jack Spade's friends. I think I shall have to raise the price on Monsieur Spade."

And so on. His attentive eye caught sight of a wrinkled-looking man hovering around the baggage loading area, making a nuisance of himself.

"Be careful with that!" he was shouting as a huge crate was being swung aboard. "Are you certain those ropes are secure? Gently, man, gently! Twenty years of my life are in that crate!"

"Humpf!" Renard sniffed. "Le Professor. I wonder what is in the crate? Books, undoubtedly. I will get nothing from him. I am surprised he could come up with the price of a ticket."

"Excuse me," a voice said, bringing Renard's attention back to the gangway. "Could you tell us where our state rooms are?"

Renard turned to eye one sad sack of a man. From the looks of his face, one of his parents had been a weasel, and his glasses were as thick as the windows on Al Capone's limousine.

"The name, monsieur?" said Renard, looking over his passenger list.

"Plotkin, Hiram Plotkin," said the man.

Renard glanced at his list, but, at the same time, he managed to ogle Plotkin's wife.

What a beauty! A strawberry blonde, ripe for the picking. But she appeared pale and depressed, glancing often at her husband with a wistful look.

Finding Plotkin on the list, Renard raised his eyebrows, then examined his tickets.

How could this frumpy weasel ever come up with the francs to go First Class? Renard wondered. Maybe he was one of those eccentrics who had invented a better mousetrap or something. It was obvious that Strawberry Blonde had married him for his money, then quickly realized that it wasn't enough.

"Is this your first time aboard ship, Monsieur Plotkin?" Renard asked with oily politeness.

"Yes," mumbled Plotkin nervously.

"It's our second honeymoon," said Mrs. Plotkin in a soft voice.

More like a last-ditch attempt to save a dying marriage, thought Renard, already slotting Mrs. Plotkin into his schedule.

Renard bowed. "You are fortunate above most men, Monsieur Plotkin," he murmured, looking meaningfully at Strawberry Blonde.

Mrs. Plotkin blushed. Plotkin only scowled.

Renard turned to a cabin boy hovering nearby. "Ronzo, show Monsieur and Madame Plotkin to Suite 36."

Renard turned back to the Plotkins. "My name is Officer Renard. I am the night watch officer on the promenade deck. If I can be of any service, please let me know. . . ."

Strawberry Blonde took note. "Thank you for your kindness," she said, offering him her hand, then smiling with pleasure as he kissed it elaborately. Renard smiled as the two walked away. He felt sorry for the weasel, but in the same thought, he looked forward to the comfort he might be able to supply the clearly deprived Mrs. Plotkin.

The cabin boy and the Plotkins had vanished, leaving Renard in a blissful reverie, when the sound of applause from the wharf caused him to snap to attention. Looking down, Renard beheld the most beautiful woman he had ever seen. Wrapped in expensive sable, her sultry features were enhanced by the twilight.

Pausing dramatically before boarding, she waved to her admirers and the photo-bugs, then turned and regally ascended the gangway. She looked up at Renard. Their eyes met. He felt a tingle up his spine and a soft burn in his stomach. Taking her hand to help her, he was lost in a beautiful dream. For a wild moment, they were drinking a champagne toast on a baroque balcony in Monte Carlo. They were stepping off the running board of a cream-colored Hispano-Suiza, waving at an opening-night audience. For just a moment, he stood in the light—the light of flashbulbs, flood lights, marquee lights.

Then China White, ethereal, beautiful, perfumed, elegant, drifted on past him, a gaggle of reporters hot on her heels. Her expensive fragrance tantalized his nose in the passing breeze.

Renard wanted her.

Someone else on board the *Normandie* also took a special interest in China White. Hearing the noise of the approaching crowd, Hiram Plotkin turned to see what all the excitement was about. At the sight of the gorgeous woman, Plotkin's bucktoothed mouth dropped open and his weasel eyes bulged through the coke-bottle specs. Anyone getting a close look at him, however, would have been chilled by the look of intelligence in his light, intense eyes; an intelligence that belied his absentminded bumpkin guise. But nobody noticed, for all eyes were on China White.

Nobody noticed, that is, except the strawberry blonde.

"Come on, Hiram," she said, poking him.

"Leave me alone!" he snapped, and there was an edge to his voice that chilled Maggie Darr. Looking at the disguised Agent 13, Maggie wondered how much of that rapt, enchanted look he gave the beautiful China White had been an act!

The cabin boy, realizing that other tips were getting away while he wasted time, said loudly, "This way, sir!" and hurried on down the corridor.

It was the first time Maggie had ever been on an ocean liner. She was awed by its size. They had already walked for what seemed like miles to reach their staterooms. With fourteen different levels, the *Normandie* was a floating city of steel. She tried to imagine what it would take to destroy this mighty ship. It seemed impossible. Surely they'd made a mistake! Nothing could harm this wonder of technology—nothing! Even as the thought crossed her mind, she realized others must have said the same thing the day they boarded the *Titanic*. . . .

Maggie would soon have been lost in the maze of corridors had not Agent 13 made her spend last night memorizing the ship's layout. 13 also knew the number of officers, crew, the procedures above deck and below, as well as the locations of the bridge, the captain's quarters, the radio rooms.

Above all, he knew every detail about China White—her concert schedule, where her suite was located, even where she had insisted they park the limousine she had brought on board.

As Maggie looked around in pleased, naive wonder at their elegant surroundings, 13's eye was drawn to a theater marquee. China's name leaped out at him. *China White, Appearing Tonight, in Concert.*

13 stared at the marquee, feeling frustrated. What could she be up to? China was such a visible personality, she would be foolish to attempt any kidnapping or overt action on her own. Her role, therefore, was that of the conductor of this grim concerto, but where was her orchestra? Who were the players? Where was the music? As he walked past *Normandie's* elegant theater, 13's eyes were drawn to the two ancient masks carved in the entry doors. They seemed to echo his confusion.

Comedy, tragedy. Life, death. Lover, enemy.

He examined the variables.

China knew the where, the when, and the how. 13 knew China.

Somehow, he had to be the sour note in her deadly symphony. And the only thing he could do was to try to force her hand, to make her afraid, to make her wonder. Backed into a corner, she might grow careless, she might make a mistake.

13 smiled grimly. The performances transpiring on board ship that night would be far more elaborate than anything being performed on stage.

20

GRIM ASSIGNMENTS

The cabin boy opened the suite door, proudly standing back for them to enter.

Maggie looked around, marveling at the beauty of the decor. The furniture was made of rich cherry wood; the lighting was soft, indirect; velvet upholestry covered the chairs; and a bouquet of lilies stood on her night table.

"Oh, Hiram! It's wonderful!" she said.

"I'm glad you're pleased" he responded flatly, glancing about the room with only technical interest.

Had it been a different time, Maggie might have been able to enjoy the plush opulence. But this mission and the danger they were in consumed her thoughts. Looking at Agent 13, thinking back to her glimpse of the ravishing China White, Maggie realized with a sinking heart that the danger she feared was not a danger made up solely of hot, spitting lead.

The cabin boy began to open up their luggage, so that he might hang their clothing in the closet.

"That won't be necessary," said Plotkin, pressing a five spot into the boy's hand.

"Thank you, sir. Dinner will be served starting at eight in the Grand Lounge. I suggest reservations. I would be happy to make them for you, if you wish."

"We'll handle them ourselves, thank you."

"As you wish. In the drawer here, you will find a book containing lists of all events scheduled for the passage, as well as all the services offered. My name is Ronzo. Should you need me, just dial room service. Is there anything else I can do for you?"

"No, we want to be alone right now."

"Very well, sir."

Maggie listened as the sounds of the cabin boy's footsteps receded.

"What do you think?" she asked 13 finally.

13 did not answer. He was checking over the room and, from the frown on his disguised face, he didn't like what he saw.

He had requested an inner cabin, but none was available at such late notice. So they'd had to make do with the room reserved by the late, unlamented Jack Spade. Apparently Spade enjoyed a cabin with lots of light. As a result, 13 had two large portholes to contend with. These looked directly out on the upper deck. Though the curtains could be shut, nothing could stop the spray of machine gun fire. The walls were paper-thin, the locks easily picked.

Agent 13 switched on the radio, and the strains of "In the Mood" filled the room. This, he hoped, would make their conversation harder to discern for the casual eavesdropper.

13 reached into his case and pulled out several photo enlargements of Dr. Fischer, taken both at the Lightning Gun's demonstration and by Benny the Eye. He held them out to Maggie.

"Fischer," he said.

Taking them from his hands, Maggie gave them a quick once-over.

"Study him," 13 admonished. "He's traveling alone. Staying in Suite 48, right down the hall from us. Spade was probably supposed to keep an eye on him."

"Fischer looks a worse weasel than you!" Maggie laughed.

13 shook his head. "Appearances are deceiving. Within that ingenuous head are stored some of the most sensitive military secrets in the world."

"Could of fooled me."

"I want you to follow him. Don't let him out of your sight. According to Benny, he's not partial to lipstick on the collar, but he might be vulnerable to tears on the shoulder. Keep up the act that we're not getting along. . . ."

"If you say so." Maggie shrugged. "But I still don't see how they plan to kidnap a man on the open sea!"

"Put no crime past the Brotherhood. Assume no feat is beyond them. Unless I am terribly wrong, they do not intend to let the *Normandie* drop anchor at Le Havre."

"O.K. I watch Fischer. Meanwhile, what will you be doing?" Maggie asked. But she already knew the answer.

"Watching China White."

Maggie smiled wryly. "Of course," she muttered.

Hearing the sarcastic tone in her voice, 13 looked up quickly. "Whatever the plot might be, rest assured that she's behind it."

"And how many are behind her?"

"There's no way to tell, but I believe it's reasonable to assume that she's not acting alone."

"Is she the Masque?" Maggie asked hesitantly.

13 thought for a moment. It was a question that had drifted through his own mind like leaves in a windstorm. The evidence all seemed to say yes, yet something wouldn't let him believe it. Something kept wanting to hold on to the memories of

innocence and love that they had shared years ago. But people change. . . .

"I believe so," he said finally, his voice flattened.

"So what can we do?" Maggie asked, feeling helpless. "Just watch Fischer? Just watch her? That isn't much—"

"Time is my enemy, her ally. Whatever the Brotherhood has planned, they are operating on a crucial time schedule. I've got to force China's hand, try to upset that time schedule if I can. To do this, I must risk everything. If I fail, responsibility for the safety of hundreds of thousands of lives will fall upon your shoulders."

Maggie's eyes opened wide. She swallowed. "What—what does that mean?"

"Under no circumstances are you to allow the Brotherhood to escape with Fischer. Kill him if necessary."

"And what about China White?" Maggie asked softly. "Will you kill her?"

"If necessary."

Ignoring Maggie's look of disbelief, 13 sat down resolutely before the large mirror and began to strip off the make-up that had turned him into the innocuous Mr. Plotkin.

As he did so, he wondered—he had killed so many without a qualm. But—could he kill her?

Fearful that China White might try to kidnap the scientist and smuggle him off the ship even before it departed, Maggie stayed out on the top deck, close to Fischer, until the gangway was pulled up.

Dr. Fischer was among the throng packed on the deck, but he was not part of it. Everyone else was waving and tossing gay spirals of colored paper down into the cheering crowd below. But the professor was staring dully at the shore, looking worried and preoccupied.

"No wonder!" muttered Maggie grimly. "Thinking about selling out your own country to the Nazis! How much are they paying you, Judas?"

The *Normandie* blew her powerful horn, a final salute of farewell to the skyscrapers of New York. The city responded with a synchronized din of auto horns and cheers as the huge ship slipped slowly backward into the Hudson River. Turning, it then made for the waiting Atlantic and, five days later, the shores of France. One by one, the escort of small yachts and planes were left behind until the *Normandie* was alone, the mighty queen of the swirling seas.

The salty breeze of the Atlantic filled Maggie's lungs as she drew a deep breath. There was no longer any turning back, she thought, watching the skyline of New York grow small. The passing waters looked cold and deep, covering unmarked graves. The mighty *Normandie* suddenly looked very small and vulnerable when compared to the vastness of the restless sea.

Fischer abruptly left the deck. Following him, Maggie saw him safely ensconced in his cabin. Then she returned to her own to report that there was, as far as she could see, no one the least bit interested in Fischer.

But Agent 13 was gone.

Sighing, Maggie propped the door open slightly, so that she could hear and see if anyone either came to or left Fischer's cabin. Then she started to change for dinner. Everything was so peaceful. For a fleeting moment, Maggie questioned the Agent's hypothesis, hoping he was wrong.

GATHERING GLOOM

Dinner was like a splendid dream that night for the passengers dining in the *Normandie*'s First Class dining room. Two hundred and eighty-two feet long, the room was capable of seating over seven hundred diners under the beneficent gaze of Athena Parthenos, Greek goddess of protection, whose thirteen-foot-tall statue stood watch over the room. The walls of the great hall were adorned with Labouret's glass slabs that rose twenty-eight feet up to the richly coffered ceiling. The "miraculous grotto," as it was termed, was lit by startling sixteen-foot sconces decorating the walls, as well as by crystal towers of light that rose in the room's center.

The dining room was a floating four-star restaurant. Since the price of the food was included in the crossing price, diners could eat themselves into oblivion on *Jambon d'York* or *Le Caneton a L'Orange*. The ladies put their diets aside when tempted with the delicacies of sweet *Patisserie* and *Glaces*, prepared in mysterious ways, to which only the French were privy.

Watch Officer Renard stood on the grand stairway that flowed into the hall, his uniform starched stiff and spotless. He scanned the busy tables carefully, then he saw her. She was not hard to find, her raven hair a beacon of darkness amid the glitter.

China White sat at a table surrounded by admirers—the entertaining Maharajah on one side, a handsome, well-known German actor on the other. It would be tough for Renard, but he liked challenges—he wasn't about to let this one slip away.

He watched her dine, entranced by her grace and elegance. Mozart's *Eine Kleine Nachtmuzik* filled the air.

As the dessert remains were taken up, Cuban cigars were lit. Courvoisier and Benedictine were served. The diners rose from their tables, many heading for the Grill Room for its wild swing dancing. But, for the more romantic couples, it was the Grand Lounge. Here they could sip life at a slower, more elegant pace, dancing to the music of seductive strings that lulled them into oneness.

Renard observed China White as she drifted from the table like an elfin spirit, her pearls and elegant Chanel gown enhanced by the beauty of her satinlike flesh. Her courtiers stood up, offering escort. She shook her head, leaving them behind as she walked toward the Grand Lounge alone. It was Renard's moment. He closed in carefully. Little did he realize, but the hunter was also being hunted.

Few rooms in history have been as elegant as the Grand Lounge of the *Normandie*. Modeled after the Hall of Mirrors at Versailles, it sparkled like an elegant jewel within a crystal box.

Four large glass reliefs by Dupas, each measuring twenty-one feet high by forty-nine feet wide, adorned the gold and silver gilt hall. Its ceiling rose thirty-one feet from the dance floor; tall rectangular windows, five on either side, opened to the "green pastures" of the passing waters. What space was left was filled by elegant mirrors .

Without knowing it, those in the Grand Lounge that night saw something only a chosen few had seen in twelve years. Yet the only ones to notice were a pair of young newlyweds.

"Who is that man? I don't recall seeing him embark," the young bride asked, eyeing a tall, handsome man dressed in a tuxedo.

"And I shouldn't be sorry to see him disembark," the groom responded, turning his young wife away, not knowing that he was one of the few ever to have seen Agent 13's true face.

It was a face unlike any other nature has chiseled. At once stunning and unremarkable, each line and curve of the face was perfect. His cheek bones were neither low nor high, his eyes were neither blue nor brown, his mouth was neither large nor small, his teeth were neither straight nor crooked. It was the perfect base on which to construct the many identities he adopted—a canvas that accepted any hue.

Yet, guiding the face was a strength of character and a charisma rarely found, a strength that showed through and could have acted as a magnet to beautiful women or theater fans or political backers, had he chosen those lines of life. But Fate had arranged differently. . . .

13's lack of disguise was purposeful. Other than Maggie Darr, there was only one person on board tonight who would recognize his real face. Recognize it and, hopefully, be startled enough by the recognition to act rashly.

Keeping near China White, Agent 13 watched in amusement as Renard made his move.

As China floated through the Grand Lounge, Renard swooped down on her like a hawk, intercepting her only paces from the dance floor. Renard had charm, there was no denying the fact, 13 thought. China smiled and laughed at

Renard's quick torrent of well-rehearsed words.

Bowing, the suave French officer indicated the dance floor. A moment later Renard's strong hands encircled China's slim waist. Clad in a skin-tight black gown, she flowed effortlessly across the floor like a dark angel, Renard guiding her gracefully. Agent 13 watched and waited.

While others danced in the Grand Lounge, Maggie Darr spent a bored evening trailing the professor. She wasn't finding it difficult to keep an eye on Dr. David Fischer. After a hurried dinner, he immediately set out for the Winter Garden Room, located near the bow of the ship. Entering the room, he sat down in a wicker chair, sipped sherry, and began to study a sheaf of papers.

"Boy, some fun evening this is gonna be!" Maggie thought, slipping into the room after Fischer was settled.

Filled with examples of prize French horticulture, the lushly planted Winter Garden Room gave an unparalleled view of the windswept seas. It was peaceful, uncrowded, suited to those who preferred the quieter pleasures of shipboard.

Trying to keep from thinking about the fun and excitement going on in the Grand Lounge this evening, Maggie sat down at a table nearby, pretending to read an account of Dame Penelope Hatford's trip up the Nile.

But her eyes covertly surveyed the room.

Soft lights fell upon a curved marbled bar that jutted out from the wall like the prow of a sleek ship. Everything in the room was done in peachy mauves, greens, and whites—gentle earth colors asking to go unnoticed amid the lilies, roses, and palms.

There were several other people in the room. In one corner, a man with a thin mustache played a baby grand piano. Fingers dancing across the ivory keyboards, he was responding to the requests of several young men sporting cream-colored blazers adorned with the Harvard emblem.

Of the other men in the room, Maggie knew one by sight, having read about him numerous times in the newspapers. His name was Nat Spencer, but he was commonly known as "the man in the iron coffin." A millionaire inventor, he had been stricken with infantile paralysis several years ago and was now forced to continue existence lying on his back in an iron lung. Only his head stuck out from the coffinlike device. Since he could not move, several small mirrors had been mounted to afford him views of the surrounding area.

Nat had refused to give in to his affliction, however. Possessed of a wry, witty sense of humor, he was a much sought-after addition to any party. With the help of two constant attendants, he went everywhere, did everything. Tonight, Nat and his "lung" rested on a wheeled cart near a table. Under the watchful gaze of a streamlined deco goddess holding a light in her hand, Nat was taking on a distinguished-looking older man in a high-stakes game of backgammon.

Other than these people, however, the room was nearly deserted. Occasionally a beautifully gowned woman and a tuxedoed man would drift in, apparently hoping to find a more "discreet" place aboard the crowded ship. Seeing them gaze into each other's eyes, watching their hands twine about each other's waists, Maggie sighed. This ship seemed to be stirring long-suppressed yearnings.

Her occasional glances about the room, however, had not gone unnoticed. They met with a surprising result. Looking back to check on Dr. Fischer, she was startled to see him staring at her!

His face twisted into a scowl. Hurling his papers down, he rose from his seat and moved directly toward her!

A red, angry face leaned into Maggie's. Crooked teeth, too tightly packed together for the small mouth, spat out words.

"You have been following me, young woman, and I don't like it!"

Blast the man! Setting her book aside, Maggie looked up at him in astonishment. "Excuse me?"

"There's no excuse! Either this situation ends immediately or I shall report you to the captain."

"I believe that you've mistaken me for someone else," Maggie said politely.

"Don't be impertinent, young lady! You've been following me all day and now I can't even drink my sherry in peace. Who are you working for?" he demanded. "The FBI?"

Maggie glanced around. He was creating a scene. The Harvard men were watching now with attentive interest, and even the older backgammon player looked up. Nat in the iron lung was watching through his mirror.

She was suddenly angry. Damn Fischer anyhow! Probably feeling guilty, and too weak and nervous to deal with it.

Coldly, Maggie rose to her feet. She would have to bluff her way out. "My name, sir, is Mrs. Hiram Plotkin, Hiram Plotkin the Third. My husband is presently taking a nap in our stateroom. If you don't quit bothering me, I'll get him, and I don't think he will take kindly to your accusations."

Dr. Fischer stared at her a moment, then—to Maggie's amazement—his face went gray. Mumbling something, he turned away, running a trembling hand through his hair.

Impulsively, feeling truly sorry for the man, Maggie reached out her hand. "Please, don't go," she said sincerely. "Look, I didn't mean that about getting my husband. He probably wouldn't care anyway. Say, are you sick or something? You don't look good. Can I help?"

Fischer looked around. "I'm sorry I bothered you," he said with a sigh. "I've been under a lot of pressure lately and I—"

Smiling, Maggie encouraged him to talk.

"I'm Dr. David Fischer," he said with belated grace, "and I would like to apologize."

"Accepted," she replied, shaking his hand.

"Would you join me in a cognac?"

She smiled. "I would."

Seeing that apparently there wasn't going to be any more action of interest, the Harvard boys, shrugging, went back to their piano. The back-gammon players returned to their game.

Maggie took a seat with Dr. Fischer. The attractive young woman proved a sympathetic listener, and soon, before he quite realized it, Dr. Fischer was pouring his heart out to her.

"The demonstration of the Lightning Gun was an astounding success!" he said. "I thought for certain that the Army would be crawling to me on their hands and knees. All I needed was a grant! That's all. Two days later—I got a letter." Fischer shook his head. "The State Department says that, although the Armed Services see the 'potential' of such a device as this Lightning Gun, they aren't interested in developing it at the present time!"

"But why?" asked Maggie curiously. "If it's as good as you say—"

"Oh, it's good!" Fischer said, tearing his hair in frustration. "But they're locked into technology rooted in the past. They want guns that fire real bullets, not light. I'm a toy-maker, a tinkerer. They don't *begin* to comprehend the power I can harness and direct!"

13 comprehends, Maggie thought uneasily. He knows this gun's deadly potential—and so does the Brotherhood! Unconsciously, her hand went to her purse.

"Twenty years of work and grants down the drain!" Fischer's head sank into his hands. "My colleagues pitied me. . . *pitied* me."

He tossed back another Cognac. How many was that, Maggie wondered—his fourth? And he probably wasn't accustomed to drinking. . . . She ought to try to get him out of here.

"But then," he said in a loud whisper, "I got a call. A scientist, very big name. Happened to be German. They're interested."

"Who?" prompted Maggie.

"The United European Defense Company. They want me to bring my gun to France for more detailed study."

Maggie frowned. Seeing her look, Fischer squirmed uncomfortably. "Oh, I know what you're thinking. I thought the same thing. That madman Hitler isn't far away. And the scientist I spoke to was German. But he swore to me that he hated the Nazis. What could I do? I agreed.

"Then"—his voice dropped—"I noticed I was being watched, followed! A paper boy on a corner, a cab driver, a man with one leg—everywhere I went, someone was behind me. But who? The Army—after they'd turned me down? The Nazis? The French? I thought it would stop on the boat, but it's started again! I've seen a man hanging around my cabin. I'm frightened! And I have nowhere to go, nowhere to turn."

His head in his hands, he began to weep.

Maggie shifted uneasily. She was only supposed to keep an eye on Fischer—now it looked like he might fall apart at the seams! She needed 13, needed him badly. But where was he . . . ?

WALTZ OF THE SPIDER

"I give you my word, beautiful lady," Renard said, looking deep into China's eyes, "you are as safe aboard this ship as you would be in your own bed. Our course takes us near no icebergs. Our radio man is in constant contact with the shore. Even in the unlikely event of a mishap—"

"I know it is silly of me to be so frightened of the ocean." China White performed the amazing trick of making her voice vulnerable and sultry at the same time. "And you are very reassuring. So, these men in the radio room, they are in constant communication with the shore? What would they do if some terrible disaster were to occur. . . ."

Renard was enchanted with her. Smiling down into those deep, dark blue eyes, he was just about to describe in elaborate detail the workings of the radio room when he felt a hand tap him lightly on the shoulder.

"May I cut in?" said a baritone voice.

Renard turned, barely able to conceal his outrage. How dare anyone interrupt him, an officer of this ship! He would brush the person off, politely but firmly. Then his eyes met the eyes of the stranger's, and Renard suddenly had second thoughts. The man's eyes were animal-like, with no trace of emotion in them. Renard had seen eyes like that only once before—in a Parisian zoo. They had belonged to a black panther.

The stranger's gaze went to Renard's dancing partner.

Startled, Renard turned to look at her as well. China White was staring at the stranger as though he truly could be a black panther! She didn't say a word, she didn't gasp or start. But she was affected by the stranger, that was certain. Her skin was pale, her eyes wide and shimmering with a radiant luster, her lips slightly parted.

Renard stepped aside. Who was this man? the officer wondered as he walked from the dance floor. He certainly would have recognized such a striking face! Perhaps the man was from the tourist class . . . Looking around the Lounge quickly, Renard saw Purser André Damour standing near the staircase, observing the gala. He would ask him. Damour never forgot a face.

China White looked at the man before her. She said nothing. What could be said when life stopped and then spun backward? Her heartbeat quickened. She stared into his eyes. Reaching up, she touched his cheek. She breathed his scent. The man was older, wiser, darker. But it was him.

The orchestra played *Tales of the Vienna Woods.*

"Touch me and wake me," she said to him.

He held out his hand. She took it.

Her hands tingled as the pulse from his hand echoed through her, beckoning for a union of two rhythms so much alike but separated for so long.

He held her, transporting them both to another place, another time.

The world disappeared around her. She had often dreamed of this moment with longing and with dread. She was suddenly unsure of herself, remembering days of lost innocence and purity, days of a wondrous, splendid love. . . .

Why had he come back now? Her soul cried in agony. Why now? The moment before the storm.

"You're alive," she whispered, pressing her cheek into his shoulder.

"Disappointed?"

"Relieved."

They drifted across the dance floor, his strong arms holding her effortlessly. She pressed herself against him. The threads of her gown couldn't hold back the passions she felt surging through her, passions she had felt for this man long ago. Could those moments be relived?

"I heard you were dead."

"Did it matter to you?"

"Yes! Oh, yes!" she admitted, her arms tightening around him.

Her words stung 13 with a thousand barbs. Was she playing him for the fool? Or was she telling the truth? And if the truth, what then? Only torment perhaps . . .

"Once upon a time" was a long time ago. . . .

Seventeen years old. Walking among the high arches and pillars of the Shrine on a moonlit night, he had glimpsed the truth, and in so doing, saw the dark heart of the Brotherhood. The horror was revealed, a dream shattered. Suddenly he realized that he had been trained for a life of evil!

For long months, he concealed his knowledge. But, of course, they found out—as they find out everything. He was a threat. They tried to silence him forever, but he had learned their lessons well, and he escaped.

She was the girl he loved. He would leave, but he would take her with him.

His heart pounded as they embraced secretly beneath the canopied trees. "They tried to kill me," he told her. "Soon, they will come for you. We must escape, tonight."

Young, frightened, unsure, they held each other in the shadowed moonlight. Their urgent whispers forged a path to the future.

"I'll meet you in the garden when the moon disappears behind the peaks," she promised.

She never came.

Instead, agents of the Brotherhood arrived, but they were late. Too late to catch 13. Hunted, he left her behind, his love poisoned by the knowledge that she had betrayed him. Never to see her again until now. . . .

The unspoken question came to his mind, the question that he had carried with him since his day of flight. "Why did you do it?" he asked. "Why did you tell them where to find me?"

As if she had been waiting for that question, she answered it with a burst of words. "They were waiting for me when I returned to the cloister! I tried to lie, but it was no use! They knew—everything!"

Her head bowed. "You know what they were capable of doing. I held out as long as I could. . . ."

He didn't answer, only held her more tightly. Finally, however, he said harshly. "Then why did you stay? After what I told you?"

"I stayed because the alternative was death." Her voice was flat, emotionless.

"Come with me now! Together we can—"

China put her hand to his mouth. She knew what he was going to say, and it was useless. The Brotherhood was too strong. It was only a matter of time before they caught up with him and crushed him.

"Please, don't! These events have a life of their own. Neither of us has the power to stop what will occur."

"And what are 'these events'?"

China White shook her lovely head. "We've

both traveled down many dark roads since then."

"Turn back," he whispered.

"It is too late."

An instant later, he felt a slight movement of her hand at his shoulder and glanced into the mirror of her eyes. A waiter melted back into the crowd. But, 13 noticed, this waiter was not waiting tables. He was doing nothing but watching them. And he kept one hand in his pocket.

13 smiled grimly. "How many more of your friends are aboard?"

"I don't know what you are talking about."

Looking down at China, 13 could almost see her mind working. He smiled again. She was in a strange predicament. As long as he was with her, no harm could come to him. A man suddenly dropping dead in her arms would attract the attention of the world. But, if she let him leave, he would melt into the crowd, assuming one of his many disguises.

So, he was not surprised to see her beautiful face turn up to his or to hear her whisper seductively, "The Brotherhood would welcome your return." She tempted his ear with the warmth and lightness of her breath. "I could arrange it."

"I'd sooner pass through the gates of hell."

"Listen to reason," she said, pressing against his chest. "You are alone against an organization that has existed thousands of years!"

"An organization that has become as rotten as a corpse."

"Definitions will reverse, history will change. The Brotherhood is strong! Soon they will rule this planet under one law, one goverment."

"How many innocent people must die first? Ten, twenty, a million?"

"It doesn't matter! The petty squabbles that have kept man a slave to himself will be broken, the end result will be a lasting peace!"

"The peace of slavery!"

"Your struggle is futile and you will die!"

"Then that is my fate. As you said, people dying doesn't matter to you. Know this, China, I am sworn against the Brotherhood and all who stand for it."

She looked into his eyes. "Including me?"

He didn't answer.

"Miss White?" a voice implored.

A frantic steward had hurried onto the dance floor and was now hovering near.

"Excuse me, Miss White. I was told to remind you—your curtain is in fifteen minutes."

"Thank you, I'll be right there."

The steward stood off to the side and waited, obviously having received instructions to come back with Miss White or not come back.

"Will you be at my performance?" The dark blue eyes looked up at him.

13 smiled. "What do you think?"

"I can't guarantee your safety unless you escort me."

13 scanned the area. The entire room seemed to be filled with eyes watching them. Whether it was because of China's beauty and celebrity or because the eyes belonged to agents of the Brotherhood, he had no way of knowing.

China waited, smiling confidently, certain of what his answer must be.

"Another time, perhaps." He had made his decision years ago and there was no turning back. To walk with her was to walk into darkness.

Disappointment and a brief flicker of anger marred her lovely face for an instant. She looked at him long and intently, as though seeing his face for the last time and wanting to memorize it. "I tried to save you," she said. "Remember that."

Then, in a barely audible voice, "I love you. I always have."

She kissed his cheek. Her warm, soft lips sent sparks through him. Then, gracefully, she turned and walked away.

The moment China White left the room, her agents began to close in. 13 could see them sidling across the dance floor, eager to get to him. China must have given them some sort of sign.

Coolly, Agent 13 walked slowly and with nonchalant grace from the dance floor. He wasn't concerned because, in effect, the cavalry was riding to his rescue. On second thought, you might say it was the French Foreign Legion. Sure enough, here came Officer Renard and the purser. He had noticed them, waiting like jackals for China White to leave. It would never do to make a scene before her. But now she was gone, and they were swooping in for the kill.

"Excuse me, monsieur," Renard said arrogantly, putting his hand on 13's lapel.

"Yes, what is it?" the Agent said brusquely, brushing the officer's hand away.

"Purser Damour would like a word with you," Renard said.

A uniformed purser stepped forward and held out his open hand. "I would like to see your cabin key, monsieur."

"Is there a problem?" 13 glowered.

"We sincerely hope not, monsieur." The purser's tone insisted that there most certainly was.

13 glanced around nervously, fingering his tie like a petty crook caught in a scam. What he was really looking for were China's agents. They had stopped in their tracks, glaring at Renard and the purser, waiting for them to leave.

13 searched his pockets and patted his jacket

once, then shrugged.

"I guess I must have left it back in my room. Damn! Now I'm locked out! Can one of you let me in with a passkey?"

"Which is your cabin, monsieur?" The purser sneered. He had heard this one before.

"Twenty-eight D"

"Twenty-eight D?" Snorting. "I'm afraid there is no such cabin."

"Well, it's been a long night, hasn't it, Officer, uh—?" 13 strained to read his name tag.

"Renard, Officer Renard."

"And I don't believe we caught your name," the purser said.

"Fredericks, J.C. Fredericks."

The purser promptly pulled out a passenger list and gave it the once-over.

"You are not listed as a passenger, Monsieur Fredericks."

"What do you mean—'not listed'?"

"It means that unless you have forgotten your name as well as your key, monsieur, you are a stowaway."

"How dare you!" 13 snarled, outraged. Several people turned to gaze at him with interest.

Renard grabbed him firmly by the arm. "I suggest that we take a walk down to Security, Monsieur Fredericks."

"I didn't pay good money to be treated like this!" 13 yelled. Now everyone in the immediate vicinity could see and hear him, which was precisely what he wanted. The more attention he attracted, the greater the risk China's agents would take in trying to get to him.

"This won't take long," the purser said.

"I'll sue! You'll be hearing from my lawyer!" 13 shouted as they hustled him out of the hall.

13 smiled grimly, catching a glimpse of the dis-

concerted faces of China's agents as the purser dragged him—still protesting—past them. They glowered at him, powerless.

Once in the safety of the foyer, Renard gave 13 a quick frisk. He halted at 13's inner coat pocket. Reaching in, he pulled out a deck of cards.

"A card man, eh?"

"Are they marked?" asked the purser.

"Probably."

"Those are your own cards from the Smoking Room! I'll have your jobs for this!" 13 snarled. "I demand to see the captain!"

"He will undoubtedly be delighted to see you, too, I am certain." Ignoring his threats, the purser turned to Renard. "Can you handle him, or do you need help?"

"No one's going to handle anybody," 13 muttered.

Renard looked at the card sharp in disgust and said something in French. The purser smiled.

"Let me know what you find out. He may be working with friends."

Renard tugged on 13's arm. "Let's go."

13 allowed Renard to pull him down the corridor. Glancing back, he saw two of China's agents in the doorway.

Lifting his hand, 13 made a quick sign to them—as though warning them away. Renard took note immediately.

"Ah, ha!" he said triumphantly, whirling to look at the agents. "So, you *are* working with someone. Purser—"

But the purser was already in hot pursuit. China's agents, looking extremely startled, were trying to melt back into the crowd.

Grinning to himself, 13 allowed Renard to drag him off.

23

FISH IN THE NET

The more Maggie was around Dr. Fischer, the more pity she felt for the nerve-shattered man. He was obviously caught up in a maelstrom of events he didn't understand.

"I've made a horrible mistake," Fischer blubbered. "I need to get to the authorities—"

A waiter with slicked-back hair suddenly appeared at their table. "Would you care for another cognac?"

"Yes, and one for the lady as well," Fischer mumbled without looking up.

The waiter wrote down the order and left.

"Is he one of the men who's been following you?" whispered Maggie.

Fischer looked up blankly. "I don't know."

"The hem on his pants is an inch too short and his shoes weren't regulation. He left your empty glass on the table. He wrote down an order any waiter worth his salt could remember. Plus he smelled like gasoline and his hands were heavily calloused and smudged with grease. I don't know who he is, but he sure isn't a waiter."

Suddenly she heard the click of a pistol's hammer behind her.

"If it ain't Sherlock Holmes," a voice hissed.

Dr. Fischer's mouth sagged open. Maggie whirled. A man was standing behind them. His bald head resembled a cue ball, and he wore a tuxedo that looked two sizes too large. Walking around the table, he jabbed a heavy pistol into the professor's spine.

"By God," Fischer moaned, "I'll report—"

"You won't do no reportin' to nobody, pal. You're comin' with us." Cue Ball nodded to the "waiter," who went to check on the exit door.

Leaning down to speak into Maggie's ear, Cue Ball mouthed, "Just keep nice and quiet, Duchess. I got others around. Yah start squawkin' and they'll drill yah."

"Don't hurt me, please!" Maggie whimpered, cringing, even as her hand went to her purse.

Cue Ball turned back to Fischer, who seemed drained of life. "Now get up, doc. We're gonna walk outta here nice an' slow."

"Iron Lung" Nat and his friend, so interested in Fischer before, now seemed completely engrossed in their game. The music being generated by the Harvard boys was loud enough to drown out anything, except maybe a gunshot.

The fake waiter, standing at the door, motioned that the coast was clear. Cue Ball gripped Fischer's coat, pulling him to his feet. "Move it."

Fischer rose like a zombie and staggered out of the room. Cue Ball looked as if he were just helping a man who had had too much to drink.

Maggie took another quick look around. Cue Ball had said there were others, but it could be a bluff. At any rate, Maggie didn't have much choice. Fischer was obviously incapable of doing anything to help himself. Making up her mind, Maggie's hand dove into her purse.

"Look out! She's gotta gun!"

Maggie fired.

The screaming slug slammed into Cue Ball's shoulder with a sickening thud. The impact spun him around. Rage contorted his face. Glaring at her, he raised his pistol.

Maggie fired again. This time the spinning lead found its mark, tearing through his throat and out the portside window.

Suddenly, it seemed, gunfire came from everywhere. Using Fischer as a shield, the "waiter" was backing out the door. Maggie hesitated. 13 had told her to kill Fischer. But how could she shoot that poor man whose only sin was being a genius ahead of his time?

As another bullet tore an arm off a Winged Victory statue behind her, Maggie hit the floor shoulder-first and rolled. That bullet had come from a different direction! Crawling to the cover of a large marble planter, she turned to see Nat's aide with a shrieking gat in his hand. And, behind him, she saw the iron lung fly open. The fake Nat crawled out, a machine gun in his hand!

Maggie risked a quick glimpse at Fischer. The waiter was dragging him out the door. But Maggie had other, more pressing problems. Nat swung the chattering automatic around. Keeping her head low, Maggie raised her pistol and fired. The bullet sent him spinning back into his iron coffin—forever. His finger tightened in death around the trigger. The machine gun's wild staccato riddled the ceiling like swiss cheese and sent the gangly aide diving for safety.

Two more shots came at Maggie from yet another direction—the bartender! The flowers above her shredded like confetti. Maggie's pistol barked, striking the mirror behind him and blowing an etched Phoenix to smithereens, but not harming the bartender. Nat's aide had regained his feet and was shooting with renewed coolness.

Maggie was trapped, caught in a crossfire of deadly lead. Chipping sounds told her the planter she was using as cover was slowly disappearing.

Hearing a yelp of terror, Maggie spun and fired. Her bullet thwacked into the splintered door frame. But it was too late. The waiter and Fischer had disappeared.

Maggie tried to get up to follow, but another bullet went zinging past her ear. She was helpless. Cursing herself for letting Fischer get away, she peered up over the planter, firing blindly at her attackers. But then her gun clicked empty.

Spitting a clip out of her gun and jamming a new one in, Maggie noticed that, suddenly, everything was quiet. She risked raising her head just in time to see the bartender scuttle out a service door. Her glance went to the iron lung. A plump arm dangled over the side, dripping blood into a crimson puddle. The aide and the other backgammon player were gone. Stunned, her ears ringing, Maggie sat back, dazed but in one piece.

Someone shouted. Then there was the clamoring of the Harvard boys pulling themselves out from behind the piano where they'd taken refuge. One of them grabbed a ship phone.

"Get me Security! There's been a shooting!" he said in a shaking voice.

People jammed in the doorway, pointing and yelling. The Harvard boys came running over to Maggie. Hurriedly stashing her gun in her purse, hoping they hadn't seen it, Maggie sank back into the corner, sobbing and wailing.

"You all right?" asked one of the Harvard men, dropping down beside her.

"It was terrible," Maggie moaned. "They just came from nowhere! They almost sh-sh-shot me."

"Who?" demanded a man in the uniform of an Army colonel, dropping to her other side.

"Gangsters! And they took my David. . . ." She wept bitterly.

"Which way'd they go, ma'am?" asked a burly

Texan.

Maggie pointed weakly to the service door behind the bar.

What followed amazed even Maggie Darr. It seemed as if every man in the room pulled a pistol, ready for pursuit. This wasn't at all what she had expected. She had to go after the kidnappers and either kill Fischer or rescue him. But when she tried to get up, one of the Harvard boys held her back.

The Texan, checking the chamber on his pearl-handled Colt .45, was already bounding out the service door, followed by the Army colonel and several Harvard boys. More people were beginning to crowd in the doorway. Maggie *had* to get out of here!

Slumping back, she let her eyes roll in her head. "Water!" she murmured.

"Water! She's going to faint!" cried the Harvard boy at her feet. Leaping up in a panic, he ran for the bar. That was Maggie's chance. Scrambling to her feet, she drew her gun. "Get out of my way," she said coldly, glaring at the shocked people in the doorway. "They've got my David, and I'm going after them!"

"She's gone mad!" wailed a fat woman in the doorway.

"That's right, sister," Maggie said grimly, walking forward. "Now I'm going to tell you once more. . . ."

People melted from the doorway. Maggie darted through, catching a glimpse from the corner of her eye of the ship's security officers dashing down the corridor.

Pressed up against the side of a bulkhead, Maggie watched as the security officers dashed inside the Winter Garden Room. Good. They'd be kept

busy in there for a while, sorting out all the stories. What with the cowboy and the soldier wandering around with guns, they probably wouldn't
come after Maggie just yet.

Satisfied, she hurried down the corridor.

Outside the immediate area surrounding the
Winter Garden Room, the rest of the ship was
quiet. Most people were either dancing, drinking,
or sleeping off the effects of one or the other. The
corridors were empty. The few people Maggie
passed appeared totally unaware that a blazing
gun battle had just been waged a few hundred feet
away. It wasn't surprising when one considered
the sheer size of the ship with its fourteen different decks and sophisticated soundproofing.

Maggie longed to find 13, but there wasn't time,
even if she had known what his present disguise
looked like. Fischer was her responsibility, anyway, and she'd failed. Running down the corridors, glancing into open doorways, Maggie
thought of reporting to 13 that she'd failed. Her
face flushed.

She had to find Fischer! But how? Her muscles
aching, her lungs burning, Maggie stopped to rest
and make herself think calmly. She couldn't
waste time dashing around the ship aimlessly. It
could take weeks to search every room. He could
be anywhere. Then—

Gasoline! She suddenly remembered. The
waiter who had escaped with Fischer had grease-
smudged hands and smelled like gasoline!

"The garage!" she said to herself. Checking the
clip on her pistol, she headed for an elevator.

24

LIGHTS OUT
FOR THE LADIES' MAN

Watch Officer Renard dragged "Mr. Fredericks" through the corridor.

"This isn't the way to the bridge," the Agent mumbled.

"No," said Renard coldly. "The captain is a most busy man. We will see him later. First, you and I have a score to settle."

Renard hauled 13 through a bulkhead door to the Promenade Deck, now deserted at night. "Your dancing days are over, my friend." Flinging the Agent up against the railing, Renard took a swing—and connected with nothing but air.

"*Mon Dieu!* What the—" He gasped.

Renard never knew what hit him. Suddenly, he was flying through the air. The cold iron of a beam sent him dribbling to the deck as his world whited out.

Agent 13 looked at his watch—the time was 11:45. China's concert would end at midnight. Even if she had been informed that 13 had escaped her agents, she would be able to do nothing until she had finished her concert. That left 13 precious time.

An elderly couple strolled by, arm in arm in the moonlight. They looked at the crumpled officer and the Agent.

"Food poisioning," the Agent said in worried tones.

The couple shook their heads in sympathy but moved on quickly, not wanting to get involved.

13 quickly heaved the unconscious Renard into one of the lifeboats. A moment later, he re-emerged, dressed in Renard's slightly rumpled uniform. By stuffing several small pieces of cotton in his upper and lower gums and slicking back his hair, 13 managed to transform himself into a passable member of the French crew. With a crew of over thirteen hundred, 13 felt little fear in being unveiled as an imposter.

Hurrying along the deck until he reached the Terrace Deck cabins, he peered through the curtained windows of the Rouen Suite. The rooms were lavishly decorated with black lacquered furniture and freshly cut lilies in crystal vases. A baby grand stood in the center of a living room.

But there was no movement.

13 pressed his ear against the chilled, smooth pane of glass. There was silence. Satisfied that the suite was empty, he entered the corridor and approached the door. He listened again . . . still no sounds. Easily picking the lock, he entered.

Normally reserved for Marlene Dietrich, the Rouen Suite had been given over to another star of equal brightness—China White.

13 padded softly through the empty rooms, searching for a clue that might reveal China's plans. Opening her closet, he quickly went through her designer gowns. Her fragrance lingered on the fragile silks, making him remember. . . . Angrily, he shook his head. There was no time for that now!

Frustrated, 13 shut the door. To all appearances, China was just what she claimed to be—an international operatic star on her way to a series of European engagements.

13 turned his attention to a black laquered desk

in her bedroom. In a drawer, he found a leather portfolio containing booking dates around the Continent. Paris, London, Rome, Milan, Berlin—all the capitals in Europe would have the opportunity of paying China White homage. Her booking agent had booked her in the finest hotels the cities could offer, and her date book showed a full schedule of dinner engagements.

Maybe I'm wrong, 13 thought. Maybe the Brotherhood has no intention of destroying the *Normandie*. Maybe they just want Fischer.

No! 13 clenched his fist. Every fiber of his being told him he was on the right track.

He could see the Masque's plans as clearly as if he had drawn them up himself. Destroy the *Normandie*, destroy the most beautiful ship afloat, kill thousands, including some of the world's most popular, beloved celebrities—and it would create a world-wide incident. Pressure would be brought to bear on America from every corner of the globe. She would be forced to give in to the Masque's demands. . . .

Suddenly, something caught 13's attention.

Scrawled at the bottom of a page, as though China had dashed it off on the first thing at hand, was a notation, 46° 14′ N x 59° 22′ W.

To the untrained observer, it was a meaningless mathematical jumble. But to a sailor, it indicated in degrees and minutes of latitude and longitude an exact position in the sea.

13 went cold. The area pinpointed by the coordinates was in the North Atlantic Drift, a point in the currents which—if he calculated correctly—the *Normandie*, with her steaming speed of 30.2 knots, would be passing in less then fifteen minutes! Was it a point of meeting—or a tomb?

13 had to act immediately. The sleeping ship had to be roused.

Spying a new electric fire alarm on the wall, 13 pulled it.

Nothing happened!

He grabbed the ship phone. The line was dead!

"Sabotage!" he muttered.

"Well, well, well. Miss White sure had you figured right, buddy."

Throaty laughter suddenly filled the cabin. 13 spun around to see two thugs from the Grand Lounge standing in the open doorway—the cold blue steel of their pistols zeroed in on his heart.

"Looks like we caught ourselves a fish," said a short, skinny thug with a misshapen nose.

"Lookin' for somethin', officer?" His friend, who looked like a prize fighter, laughed. He had a massive lower jaw and a spudlike growth on his balding head.

"Somethin' to write your will with maybe?" commented the skinny one.

13 gave them an indignant glance. "I was delivering flowers to Miss White—"

"Stash it," said Spud, cocking his handgun.

"We search him now or when he's dead?" The skinny one grinned.

"Dead."

"Bon Voyaage, skipper." They raised their pistols. Suddenly, the room exploded with thundering crackles and flying particles.

It was as if twenty guns had opened up at once. Glowing fragments whizzed and ricocheted through the room as 13 activated the special fireworks cufflink Ray Furnow had designed for him.

"We're surrounded!" yelled Spud, diving beneath the couch for cover, while the skinny guy turned, trying to avoid the fire.

The Agent sprang at the skinny one like a leopard, hitting him on the bridge of his nose. Bone and cartilage gave way as he gave a throaty, inarticulate cry and collapsed.

13 grabbed the pistol and spun around. He wanted the other one alive. Searching the smoke-filled room, he saw a glimmer of iron—the barrel of a gun sticking out from behind a nearby couch. He kicked. A fat hand turned to jelly from the bone-crushing impact. The gun flew across the carpet.

"I want answers!" 13 demanded, pulling the thug out in the open and shoving the barrel of the .38 into his nose.

"Go take a—"

13 gripped Spud's smashed hand. Sometimes, the threat of a bullet wasn't enough.

Schooled by the Brotherhood in the months before he got away, 13 knew the various pressure points on the body and he knew just how to put them to the most effective use. . . .

With just a flick of his wrist, the Agent sent overwhelming waves of anguish through Spud's central nervous system. 13 knew from grim experience what the hood was feeling—everything in his body would suddenly turn to white-hot searing pain. Even the roots of his own hair would feel like crimson nails being driven through his scalp.

"What's going to happen?"

"This—this tub's going down," Spud moaned.

"How?" demanded the Agent.

Suddenly, a shot cracked through the room. The bullet thudded into the skull of the thug, spraying 13 with blood and brains. Flinging the body to the floor, the Agent whirled around in time to see a fleeting shadow pass the window.

He looked at his watch. The minutes were ticking by. "This tub's going down. . . ."

Agent 13 hurried down the outer Promenade Deck to the central telegraph office. He jerked open the door, and his nostrils were stung by the stench of burning rubber and smoldering death.

The radio operator, a fresh bullet wound in his temple, was slumped over a blood-splattered radio table, his finger still frozen on the touch pad. Two other officers, in red-speckled whites, lay motionless behind a smashed transformer. 13 ran back out the door.

There would be no S O S from the *Normandie*.

13 dashed up a staircase leading to the Sundeck. Leaping the stairs in fours, he passed an elderly couple he vaguely remembered seeing on the dance floor.

Making a grab at the white-uniformed 13, the man mumbled, "Pardon me, Mon' Capitan, but our phones don't—" 13 was gone before he could finish, hearing the man mutter, "Typical French," as he ran past.

13 sprinted along the upper deck, the cold sea air whipping at him. Passing the smoke stack, he hurried to the stairwell, was down in two leaps, and jerked open the door to the bridge telegraph room. It was the same scene repeated. Five men dead, all the equipment destroyed.

Adrenaline pulsed through his system as he hurried past the carnage to the bridge. It was empty, cold, and deserted. The sea winds howled freely through the broken windows that had been raked and shattered with machine-gun fire.

Three officers lay dead across the white, grilled metal of the steering platform. An acidic yellow smoke drifted slowly from the shattered equipment like a spectral reaper coming to lay claim to the deceased.

The only hint of life came from the frantic voice of the engineer. Down below in the engine rooms, he was shouting into the tube, demanding confirmation of the strange orders he had received to stop the engines.

"Disregard the command!" 13 shouted. "And get someone up here to steer this thing!"

"What? Who is this?" the voice from below yelled.

"Everyone here has been killed! The ship is in danger! Send an S O S, if you can."

"Who is this?"

"A friend." 13 replaced the tube.

Pilotless, the *Normandie* steamed on into the misty night. 13 hurried out to the deck. The sounds of music and laughter echoed from a distant deck, while the silhouettes of embracing lovers could been seen near the bow. Even the waters and gusting winds had calmed, as if granting the doomed ship a moment of respectful silence.

It was ironic. Before him, he could see passengers and crew, drinking and partying the night away. Behind him lay the bullet-riddled corpses of the people responsible for their safety.

Suddenly, the night air carried the faint, incessant drone of an aircraft engine! 13's heart leaped.

He scanned the moonlit skies, searching for the source. Nothing. Yet the droning grew louder.

Then he saw it—not in the skies, but in the frigid, calm waters—a sleek, black shape skimming rapidly over the water's surface on pontoons, approaching at a speed of over one hundred miles an hour!

"A Flying Mosquito Boat!" 13 muttered grimly. He could see the torpedoes resting beneath the fuselage of the sleek prototype airboat.

The Masque's plot was now all too clear.

WHEELS OF FURY

A suave officer was more than happy to give the vibrant strawberry blonde directions to the garage. As the elevator she was riding stopped at C-Deck, Maggie left it cautiously, not knowing what to expect. The gun was back in her purse, but she had the latch open. All she saw was the closed post office and a photo studio.

Continuing past, Maggie came to an iron stairwell that led to the other five decks below.

Her high heels softly clanged on the black metal steps as she descended into the garage on the D-Deck. The gleam of night security lights shone on the highly polished hoods of expensive limos and sports roadsters.

A sudden chill wind whipped through her shimmering gown. Maggie smelled sea water.

Strange, she thought, picturing what she could remember of Agent 13's plans for the ship. There was no access to the open deck this far below the main decks! Walking around a support wall, Maggie came to another staircase. The sea wind blew much stronger here. Maggie drew her pistol and descended silently.

Reaching the greasy deck, she stumbled over a body—a mechanic, dead. Then, suddenly, she heard the hum of a freight elevator and, above that, the din of an aircraft engine.

Retreating into the shadow of a '36 Rolls, Maggie watched as a freight elevator brought a large crate up from below. Several men in cheap, well-worn suits maneuvered the crate off the elevator, loaded it onto a dolly, and then rolled it along the center aisle to the chamber beyond.

They wheeled the crate right past her hiding place. Maggie stared at the crate intently as it went by. A label, plastered to the side, was clearly visible—"Dr. David Fischer."

The Lightning Gun!

Where was 13? Maggie wondered as she followed the sinister figures through the growing pall of darkness. She didn't have to worry about making noise. The heavy crate rumbled over the concrete and metal floor as they shoved it hurriedly along. The wind grew stronger. Sneaking around a bulkhead, Maggie finally saw its source.

The auto embarkation doors were open!

Ducking behind a Cadillac, she studied the scene. Moored in the waters beside the liner was the strangest-looking airplane Maggie had ever seen. The teardrop-shaped fuselage of the sleek black craft was well above the water, supported by two pontoons affixed to struts on the craft's underbelly. It had no wings, yet it was moving at an incredibly fast speed.

The forward section of the fuselage—the pilot's compartment—was a clear Plexiglas dome. A 35-millimeter cannon protruded from its nose. A large pusher propeller provided the craft with the propulsion needed to keep up with the *Normandie*'s 30-knot speed.

An airboat, a seaplane? What was this thing? Maggie couldn't tell, and she didn't really care. Only one thing was clear—its purpose.

She watched as the figures transferred a large, ruglike bundle along pulley lines they had rigged up to an open cargo door in the craft. They were having a difficult time due to the choppiness of the seas.

A figure stepped into the light, issuing orders, and the bundle finally reached the plane safely. Dressed in a black leather flight suit, the figure turned and gave orders to prepare the crate for transfer. Her face came into the light. China White! Maggie fought back the urge to unload a full clip of lead.

Then Maggie's gaze saw something move behind the beautiful woman. There, bathed in the harsh glare of a bare light bulb, stood Dr. Fischer.

Clearly a broken man, he huddled in a corner. No one paid the least bit of attention to him. If he had any guts, Maggie thought angrily, he could escape. But he just stood there, a dull, vacant look in his eyes. Her hand tightened around the grip of her gun. He'd just signed his own death warrant.

Maggie continued to scan the scene anxiously. China White was here. Surely 13 must then be here, too. But if so, where? He could be one of the men loading the crate into the plane. He could be one of those thugs standing next to China White. Or, he might be dead. . . .

Maggie didn't know, and she couldn't count on finding him. She had her mission. But there were seven of them, she saw, counting hurriedly, and only one of her. What could she do?

Peering at the thugs and China through the window of the Cadillac that she was using as cover, Maggie suddenly had her answer—the keys of the Caddy were in the ignition!

She mentally put her "targets" into priorities. Fischer and his Lightning Gun came out on top.

Quietly, she opened the car door. The handle made a loud click, but she doubted if anyone could hear it, not over the sounds of the surf and the whirring propeller.

Sliding into the seat, Maggie started the quiet engine. No one noticed the small plume of exhaust that rose from the tailpipe. Backing the car out of the stall, she braked and brought it around. The crate with the Lightning Gun lined up nicely with the Caddy's hood ornament, she thought as she slammed the pedal to the floor.

By the time the thugs saw the Cadillac, Maggie had its speed up to over thirty miles per hour. Shouts and curses rippled through their ranks as one of them—the waiter from the bar—whirled around with a Thompson, pointing it at the vehicle hurtling toward them. The staccato of his kicking barrel lit the garage in a flash of flame.

Maggie gripped the wheel tightly, not letting up as hot blasts of lead tore the Cadillac's body to shreds. The needle on the speedometer showed forty, forty-five, then fifty miles an hour!

More pistols were drawn and shots fired. The windshield splintered into a thousand fragments. But Maggie, ducking down behind the wheel, drove on, ignoring the hundreds of pinpoint wounds. Her eyes burned like coals in the darkness as bullets slapped through the leather seat around her.

Faster and faster she drove, her foot frozen on the pedal. Her mind flashed to other places, other events. Time took on a quality of slow motion as images of people she had once known flashed before her.

She saw Jimmy, the man she had once loved, who died at the hands of Lucky's gang, then 13, a man of mystery, who had rekindled the flame of passion she believed extinguished forever. Was this death, she wondered, speeding closer and closer. . . ?

Splintering wood and snapping shards of metal and glass showered down upon her like rain. The

Cadillac bounced and lifted into the air as it thundered into the crate containing Dr. Fischer's Lightning Gun.

Sparks and smoke trailed from the undercarriage as the Cadillac plowed through the remains of the death device, plus two thugs who had failed to leap out of the way at the last minute.

A moment later, Maggie opened her eyes. She was alive. Then the fumes of spilling gas tickled her nostrils. Grabbing her pistol, she kicked open the battered door and rolled to the ground, preferring to meet the thugs' curtain of lead than to roast alive in a '37 Caddy.

Battered and bruised, Maggie dragged herself through the oil and grime of the garage floor as a series of jarring explosions buckled the steel deck. A wave of heat and concussion blasted her. Shielding herself from the blazing inferno, Maggie looked back. She could just barely make out the ruins of the Lightning Gun and the Caddy amidst the flame and smoke.

Beside her, she heard a low moan. Turning to look, she saw Fischer, huddled motionless several paces away, staring at his flaming gun in horror. Staggering to her feet, Maggie saw China's men scrambling around the burning gun—trying to save it from the all-consuming flames.

Seeing them occupied—at least for the moment—Maggie lurched over to the professor. A glazed look filled Fischer's eyes. She shook him, but there was no response beyond that moaning sound. Drugged! she thought. Raising her gun, she aimed it at him. Then shook her head. No, she couldn't kill him. Not yet. Not as long as they had a chance.

Grabbing Fischer by the coat collar, Maggie dragged him to an alcove. Suddenly, the gunmen saw them. Bullets ratatated off the steel walls like rain dancing on a tin roof. Maggie crouched low and fired twice in rapid succession. One of her bullets bit into the arm of an advancing thug, as two others returned her fire.

The hot blasts of their lead kissed her hair as she fired twice more and missed. Only two shots left. She was trapped.

The three uninjured henchmen must have had the same thought. They now advanced with reckless abandon, the blackened muzzles of their tommy guns glistening by the light of the still-blazing Caddy.

Maggie looked down at the catatonic Dr. Fischer beside her. She had no choice. At least, she knew he wouldn't suffer. Drugged as he was, he'd never know what hit him. Aiming, she gritted her teeth and prepared to carry out her assignment.

IRON FISH OF DEATH

Agent 13 clutched the lifeboat's railing with one hand. In the other, he held the pearl handle of a Colt .45. Assisting him from above, operating the winch to lower the lifeboat, stood the burly Texan, the Army colonel, and several cheering Harvard boys.

Directly below him, he could see the startled face of the Mosquito's pilot staring up at him, cursing. 13 fired into the craft. The window was bullet-proof, but not the alloy skin of the craft. Other bullets hailed down on it as the Army colonel opened up.

13 could see the embarkation door on the *Normandie* now. There was a blazing fire there, along with the blackened skeletons of a car and what looked like Fischer's Lightning Gun. Good, 13 smiled grimly. Maggie had done her job well.

But he couldn't take time to wonder how or where Maggie was. He could see the pilot yelling at someone on board the *Normandie*. Reading his lips, 13 knew the pilot was shouting that he would have to get out of there or risk being blown out of the water.

Several thugs appeared at the embarkation door, tommy guns trained on 13. The Agent aimed the .45 carefully and fired. A thug slumped forward and fell into the water.

The pilot throttled up and motioned to someone

on board as his men prepared to cut away from the pulley lines holding them to the *Normandie*.

A figure clad in black leather grabbed hold of a wheeled device and slid across the pulley lines from the *Normandie* to the Mosquito with the grace and daring of a circus preformer. Bullets from above pinged the waters around the fast-moving shape. But it was 13's shot, and he knew it.

He took a cold, deadly bead on the target, applying slow pressure to the trigger. Suddenly he saw a flash of raven black hair. China White! Something screamed from deep inside him, but the impulse commanding his finger to fire had already been sent from his brain.

13 twitched his shoulder. It was all he had time for, but it pulled back his shot. His bullet missed her by inches.

China looked back at him briefly, her eyes cool, her face beautiful. She smiled. . . .

With a strange kind of fascination, 13 watched as she slid through the cargo door in the craft.

Shaking his head, as though to break a spell, 13 turned attention back to the *Normandie*. One of the thugs was attempting to grab hold of the line while the other two were struggling with each other behind.

13 was taking aim when suddenly the line fell away from the airboat. Staring in horror, the thugs realized that they were being left behind. Their hoarse protests were answered by the Mosquito's barking machine guns. China had no intentions of leaving her men behind . . . alive.

The Mosquito turned, heading out to sea. Beneath its belly hung the torpedoes.

The Agent counted the seconds left before his motorized lifeboat could reach the waves, before he could set off in pursuit of the airboat.

Suddenly, 13 became aware of two other figures standing in the *Normandie*'s open embarkation door. One was Dr. Fischer—he saw the man shake his head groggily. The other figure was Maggie Darr. The Agent watched as Maggie raised her gun. He looked to see her target—China White.

Standing in the open cargo hatch of the airboat, China White looked up at Maggie. The blonde eyed the sultry, raven-haired adversary and coolly aimed her weapon.

"Don't shoot!" shouted Agent 13.

Did Maggie hear him and ignore him? Or was she unable to hear his voice over the roar of the aircraft engines? 13 never knew. Maggie fired her last two shots at China White.

The first shot missed, but the second found its mark. China's body jerked back hard, sliding back into the blackness of the craft's interior.

13 shrieked out something incoherent. Maggie, dropping the spent pistol to the debris-covered deck, stared up at 13 in shock, her strawberry blonde hair whipping around her face in the wind.

But then 13 felt the splash of water beneath the hull of his frail craft. He had no more time to waste. Signaling to the men up top to release him, he started the motor.

13 knew the lifeboat's speed was no match for the Mosquito's. But he'd been fighting the odds all along.

13 was familiar with the prototype airboat. He knew that the Mosquito would never be able to take off from the surface of the water until after it had discharged its two 1,200-pound torpedoes. It would need a long approach toward the *Normandie* in order to assure itself of enough airspeed for lift.

13 watched and listened as the swift craft skimmed along the surface and disappeared toward

the shimmering, moonlit horizon.

He silenced his motor and stared at the black waters, listening for the prop sounds—the noises that would tell him the trajectory of the craft and, ultimately, of the torpedoes' approach.

It was a strange silence. Only the lapping of the chilling waters could be heard beneath his hull. 13 and this frail lifeboat were all that stood between the torpedoes' explosive warheads and the *Normandie,* a quarter of a mile away.

He glanced back at the great ship. Her lights shimmered peacefully off the waters in painted streaks. The only clue to the tragedies that had struck this night was a small fire seen through the still-open embarkation door.

Agent 13 looked at the sky. The night was clear. The Milky Way, with its millions of stars, streaked across the chilled night's air like the stroke of a paint brush wielded by the hand of God.

Then 13 heard it. It made a buzzing sound at first, like the insect it was named for, but that quickly grew louder. 13's trained eyes spotted the diminutive shape coming out of the north. Firing up the lifeboat's motor again, he set his course, a bearing that would deliberately take him on a collision course with the Mosquito!

It was his only chance—to slam into the craft before its torpedoes could hit the water.

13 throttled the engine as hard as he could, hoping that by the time the pilot saw the low profile of his craft it would be too late.

The deadly Mosquito approached, its propeller giving a screaming whine of death. Closer and closer it came . . . 2000 yards . . . 1500 yards . . . 1000 yards. It kept coming, straight ahead. They hadn't seen him yet. Then he saw a flash of flame from its nose, and, a quarter of a second later, he heard the explosion. The 37-millimeter nose can non. . . .

No sooner did the thought register, than the bow of his launch exploded in a splintering ruin. A direct hit.

But it was too late for the Mosquito! It had built up so much speed that it couldn't avoid the sinking lifeboat, not without doing a nose dive into the sea! Quickly, the pilot launched the torpedoes, then, relieved of their weight, pulled the plane up in a climbing turn.

The plane nosed up toward the moon. 13 spared no time looking at it as it roared by, almost knocking him overboard, as he stared into the sea, into death, watching the bubbling wakes of the torpedoes close in on his craft.

DEAD IN THE WATER

A large crowd of pensive crew and passengers stood on the Main Deck, their eyes trained on the inky blackness to the north. Maggie, still standing near the open embarkation door, couldn't see them. Behind her, various medical personnel and assistants were trying to save some of the wounded. She was dimly aware of someone leading Dr. Fischer away.

The night suddenly turned into a horrifying day as two bright orange bursts of light flared from the ocean.

BLAA-BLAAAAM!

The concussions of the two simultaneous explosions hit Maggie an almost physical blow. Above her, she could hear the sounds of cheering.

"He did it!" whooped a voice with a Texas accent.

The Mosquito roared out of the blackness, thundering up over the stacks of the *Normandie*. Maggie heard gunfire—apparently the Army colonel was shooting at the plane. But he must have missed—Maggie could hear the engine of the plane drone on.

"Nazis!" shouted a voice.

A solicitous officer appeared beside her. "Please, my dear, allow me to assist you—"

Glancing at him, Maggie's eyes focused on one thing—his binoculars. Reaching out, she grabbed hold of them and jerked them away with a force that nearly strangled the man. Ignoring his cry of protest, Maggie lifted the powerful binoculars to her eyes.

Her hands shaking so that she could barely focus, Maggie scanned the waters where the torpedoes had exploded. She could see clearly the oil and the burning wreckage of the lifeboat.

Then, slowly, as she still stood there, the fire died. Darkness fell.

Maggie Darr stared out to sea, tears running unheeded down her face. There was no trace of Agent 13.

A kindly hand patted her shoulder. "I'm afraid no one could have survived that explosion, my dear," said the officer gently.

Maggie was overwhelmed at that moment by how much she loved the man who had sacrificed himself to save the thousands aboard the *Normandie.*

She had saved Dr. Fischer, and 13 had thwarted the Brotherhood's plan to perpetrate another disaster. But, oh the cost had been dear!

Then Maggie heard screams from the deck above.

"U-boats!" cried someone. "The Nazis are everywhere! Head for the lifeboats."

"*Sacre Bleu!* What imaginings!" swore the officer. Leaving Maggie, he headed for the Main Deck. But panic soon seized the ship. People were sighting submarines, destroyers, even icebergs. But Maggie knew the danger was over.

Later, there would be an investigation. It would produce no solid answers. All that was known was that many had died and two passengers had strangely disappeared—China White, for whom the world mourned, and a meek, mousy little man named Hiram Plotkin.

Maggie stood on the windswept deck, her hands gripping the railing as she stared at the now-silent, cold, black sea. Tears welled in her eyes, as the sea winds reddened her cheeks and blew back her hair.

After a moment of silence, she whispered, "Good-bye."

The world fell out of focus.

She dried her eyes.

Then, placing her handkerchief in her purse, she caressed the cold metal of her gun.

She would carry on, somehow trying to ease her grief with vengeance.

Is Agent 13 dead? Can Maggie carry on the fight alone?

What was in the mysterious bundle transferred onto the Mosquito?

Look for Book #2 - *Agent 13™ and the Serpentine Assassins!*